WHISPER
THROUGH THE
PAIN

THE WHISPER SERIES

LOVE IS ONLY A WHISPER
WHISPER THROUGH THE PAIN

RENEE WYNN

Whisper
THROUGH THE PAIN

BOOK TWO OF THE WHISPER SERIES

To my husband, Michael, who is the wind at my back.
I love you with all my heart.
To our beloved son, Derek,
I miss you with every breath I take.
May the angels in heaven keep you smiling.

CONTENTS

Chapter One

Melissa rummaged through the papers, scattering them over her desk. "Damn. Joan!" she shouted through the open door. Her assistant, a tall salt-and pepper-haired, middle-aged woman with pale skin and a calm disposition came into the office.

"Yes."

Melissa spared her a short glance and returned to filtering through the stacks of folders. "Do you know where the Lakeland file is?"

"Jake has it."

Melissa glared at the bundle in the assistant's hand. "What's that?"

Joan pushed them in front of her face. "Invitations to galas, parties and political events."

Melissa frowned. "I don't do social events." She grabbed the stack and threw them on her desk without thought.

Joan picked up the discarded papers and arranged them into neat piles. "You have no choice."

"We all have choices." Melissa's tone was sarcastic but she didn't care. None of those invites were for her. They only wanted Jake Sorensen, the CEO and Founder of the Sorensen Group to attend, not his right hand person. However, some thought it would be advantageous if they went through her. But right now she wasn't feeling it. Lack of sleep and working non-stop had pushed her patience to the brink of the cliff. Negotiating the Lakeland Project required a lot of concentration and hard work. She didn't want to lose the account. No mistakes were allowed. "I'm not responding," she said.

"Jake will—"

"I don't care. Where is he anyway?"

"In his office. He's in a meeting and asked not to be disturbed."

An eyebrow lifted. "Really?" She stood and moved from around the desk. "Who's with him?"

"A representative from an engineering group out of Chicago."

Melissa frowned. "Chicago? I didn't know we were working on a new project. The Lakeland acquisition along with all the other ventures are huge enough. All our concentration is supposed to be on getting the final contracts signed. He knows old man Lakeland is getting cold feet about selling." She headed toward the door.

"How do you want me to respond to these invitations?" Joan called out as Melissa walked out of the office.

"Don't," she threw over her shoulder.

"You know if there is no response they'll just keep coming."

Melissa sighed, turned around and took a few steps back to her assistant and held out her hand. Joan gave her the stack. She quickly glanced through them, picked out three, and handed the rest back to Joan.

"Okay." She waved the three invites in Joan's face. "I want you to look at these, choose one and respond with an acceptance. Ignore the others. If there's no response, they will get the message."

"But—"

"Trust me." Melissa threw her a quick wave and left the room. "They won't send another."

With hurried steps, her heels clicking on the Italian marble floor, she strolled into the hallway. With respect she acknowledged people as they greeted her.

For the last four years, she'd worked for the Sorenson Group. When she left Dallas with an unused college degree, a broken heart and a social pedigree that was of no use, she didn't know where she was headed. After months of hiding out in a college friend's remote family estate, located in the Sierra Mountains, she made her way to Los Angeles.

The first job she applied for was at Sorenson. It helped her low esteem and boosted her confidence. Especially when she received a call a few days later that extended an offer to become an apprentice in training. The company's financial wizard had taken a chance on her. Grateful for the opportunity, she accepted the apprenticeship. Within three years Melissa had moved up in the company, becoming one of the four chief negotiators for many of the acquisitions and mergers.

At Jake's office, at the far end of the floor, she knocked once and walked in. Jake stood. He frowned as she moved further into the room and shut the door.

She smiled, knowing he hated to be interrupted when he asked not to be disturbed.

"Hi Jake. Am I disturbing you?" she asked with a grin satisfied with his reaction.

The Sorenson Group, a multi-million dollar, large Capital Venture Company that bought other companies and then after a length of time, sold them for a profit, was headquartered in downtown Burbank, twelve miles outside of Los Angeles. The office complex covered two entire blocks with fifteen floors and twelve hundred employees. With branches in Seattle, San Francisco, and Boston, the company had risen to be a powerful force in the business world.

"Does it matter," he retorted, drily.

She chuckled. Since Jake could tend to be a bit of a stuffed shirt at times, throwing him off his routine was something she enjoyed.

He was a tall man with black inky hair, with the tips lying against his collar, and piercing gray eyes. His mouth was wide and sensual. He rarely smiled but when he did the entire atmosphere around him changed. Without a doubt, he was a man's man. Just looking at him caused her heart to flip and her vagina to pulsate. Now wasn't the time to be thinking about him like that, but damn she couldn't help herself.

He placed his hands on his hips. His muscular arms moved against the fabric of his starched white Brooks Brother shirt. He was physically toned from many summers felling trees for his grandfather's lumber company in Oregon. Nowadays he kept in shape running miles every day and lifting weights a few times a week.

He grew up wealthy, made no excuses for it, and worked harder than any person she knew. Dutifully he graduated from college. A couple of years later, at the age of twenty-three and not wanting to go into the family business, he started his own company. Fifteen years later, Sorensen Group was the number one venture capitalist firm in the United States. Without tapping into his trust fund or his family's wealth, Jake became a success on his own.

Jake had a mesmerizing pull when it came to business...and women. He was extremely handsome and smart. Added with the combination of being rugged and masculine, he was what her friends called a babe magnet. It didn't matter he was married, women still swarmed around him like bees waiting to mate. In droves, they vied for his attention wanting the chance to apply their stinger. He always seemed perturbed by the attention, and angry at the boldness of women's antics to get him into their bed.

Men loved his sharp mind but feared his tenacious ambition to devour competition by winning at any cost.

The man seated in front of the desk also stood and faced her. Shock riveted through her body and she stumbled in her approach.

"Melissa." The man hurried toward her. "Oh my God, Melissa." He wrapped her in his arms, as if he didn't want to let her go. He pulled back a little, his blue eyes exploring her face, but kept his arms firmly around her. "It's been so long." He kissed her forehead, then her face and her lips, lingering longer than necessary.

She groaned at the rapid emotions vibrating through her body. He deepened the kiss and she clung to him. Anger, confusion and finally euphoria at being in his arms enfolded in its grip. She moved further into his embrace, absorbing his heat and strength. Emotions long buried rose in her. Panic assailed, stemming from the sensations he'd produced—memories he'd awakened—so vivid. Things she tried to forget. She remembered the heartache—the agony of him discarding her. Shaking her head, she needed to step away but he held her hand, not letting her go.

They remained connected. So she barreled back into his arms— deeper this time. Her eyes filled with tears, distress, his with regret. Many emotions were running through her. Love—confusion— happiness—hurt—and anger. They seized her along with grief. Her insides knotted against the warring tides.

Her fingers feathered his face to make sure he was real. It was warm and caused her to tingle with sensation, making her smile at memories not forgotten. Swimming in the lake behind his parent's massive estate, the uncontrollable passion and eating ice cream in bed oblivious to the mess they made.

Melissa's breath caught in her chest when she remembered the first time they made love. It happened on her twentieth birthday, in a field of lilies and daffodils surrounded by the bright sun and the wind gently swaying the flowers.

The strength in his jaw still pronounced, just as it was all those years ago. Drawn, she wrapped her arms around him and laid her head against his chest. She shut her eyes and inhaled deeply the expensive Valentino cologne he always wore. The scent tickled her nose and she sighed with pleasure.

She stepped back and observed him for a long moment, recalling their marriage when she was twenty-two. It lasted only a few months. She'd loved this man with all her heart, body and soul— but he had almost destroyed her.

With Jake...my God. How could she have forgotten he was in the room? She shook her head to clear the fog and pulled at her hand in a panic. He held on. She tugged harder. Finally, he released her and she stepped back, creating space between them, breathing hard for air.

She turned to face Jake. He was positioned in front of his desk, leaning against it with his arms crossed and glaring hard at her. The tic in his cheek worked overtime.

Embarrassed with shame, she cleared her throat. The red tinge to his face was clear evidence of his anger along with the tightening of his lips. His stormy orbs shot daggers at her. She struggled to walk toward him; her ankles felt as if they were clasped with ten pound weights. Each step caused breathing to become difficult.

"Jake," she said, voice low and urgent to her ears, she searched for words to explain what had happened, but couldn't. She touched his arm.

He jerked, putting space between them. He scowled while he held her captive with a scorching stare.

"I can explain."

"Really?" His tone cold and hard ricocheted throughout the office.

He'd never spoken to her in such a harsh manner—not ever.

"If you would give—"

"Tell me why the hell my wife is kissing a man like he was her last drink of water?" he shouted.

CHAPTER TWO

His body screaming with tension, Jacob "Jake" Sorenson fixed his eyes on his beautiful wife. Her face was fine boned, her shiny, dark brown hair laid against her shoulders. He loved the silky, loose strands that cascaded around her face. The smoothness of her mocha skin never failed to entice him no matter where they were. She had no idea how much power she had over him.

The man with whom he was discussing a potential venture now stood beside Melissa. He touched her shoulder and Jake gritted his teeth to keep from knocking him on his ass.

A frown framed the man's face. "You're married?" he asked Melissa. His tone held bewilderment and something else Jake couldn't pinpoint—jealousy?

"Yes, Brent. Jake and I were married three months ago."

"I see." He looked at Jake with envy. "I didn't realize Melissa was married but—"

"No, Brent. Don't. I'll tell him."

Melissa took a deep breath. "This is Brent Sinclair—."

"I know who the hell he is. What I want to—"

"He's my ex-husband."

Fierce shock and then anger steamed to life hard and fast at the announcement. "Ex-husband? You never mentioned to me you were married before."

"You never asked."

"Is that your damn excuse? I never asked?" He ran a hand through his hair to ease the tension. "We talked about everything but your family. I respected your wishes because you said you were estranged from them. Not once did you say anything about a marriage."

"It was a long time ago. It wasn't something I wanted to bring up."

"Well, the way your lips locked, the memories are still alive and kicking."

"Don't, Jake. That's not the way it was." She glanced at Brent. "I haven't seen him in five years. It was the shock...of seeing him—that caused a reaction."

Brent moved near her. "I think it would be better if I left. There's a lot you and Sorenson need to discuss. But, I'm not leaving town right away." He studied Melissa for a long moment. "We need to talk. I need to—try to explain."

"It's in the past, Brent."

"Please." He took her hand. "I need to do this."

She gave him a short nod.

Brent turned to Jake and stuck out his hand. He ignored it. "Look, Sorenson, I know you're upset."

"You don't know a damn thing about me."

"You're right. I'm sorry you had to find out this way. Like

Melissa said it was a long time ago. She and I grew up together. Even though we're divorced, she's always been family and will remain so."

Was this man trying to tell him Melissa would always be a part of his life? Like hell.

"Get the hell out of my office, Sinclair."

"I'll leave but not because you commanded it. I don't want Melissa upset any more than she already is." Brent tilted her chin, looking deep into her eyes. "If you need me—"

"My wife doesn't need a damn thing from you." He pointed to the door. "This reunion is over."

Brent glanced at Melissa once again, walked out the door, closing it loudly behind him.

The silence settled thick in the room. Jake stared at her, unable to believe what had transpired in his office. He wondered what other secrets she was hiding. He hardened his resolve against the tears that filled her beautiful brown eyes, moved away, and went to stand at the office windows looking at passing cars and people walking the streets carefree and happy, while his marriage was falling apart—no it was his life—because whether he wanted to admit it or not, Melissa was his life. His heart forced him to that conclusion a long time ago.

"Jake, please look at me," she said, softly.

He didn't move.

"Please," she whispered.

He turned around. Her luminous eyes were troubled and filled with confusion. He spent a long moment devouring everything about her, memorizing the smoothness of her delicate skin, her nose and the contour of her small face. But it was her lips that were engrained in his mind. This morning, for the first time, she had straddled his lap and took him in her mouth. It had surprised him but also gave him ultimate pleasure. Sex between them was always explosive. Although many times he'd given her oral, he never pressured or asked her to do the same.

Her voice was gentle and pleading. The sound drew him into its cocoon but he fought against it. He needed a drink—real bad. There was nothing in the small cooler embedded on the wall but water and organic juices. Another company rule he had made and wished he hadn't—no liquor on the premises. Damn. He could go for a shot of whiskey.

She walked to the cooler and retrieved two bottles of mineral water. Handing him one, she unscrewed the cap and took a long swallow.

As if she knew what he was thinking, she said, "You don't have anything stronger."

He drained the water within a few gulps and threw the empty bottle in the trash can beside his desk. He gazed at Melissa as she sipped and shook his head. "Is this where we pretend you didn't kiss him and that everything is going to be fine?"

It wasn't how he'd imagined they would end up. They'd spent almost two years dating, making love, and getting to know each other—or rather, that was what he thought. He didn't know her at all.

"No. I just want you to listen...please."

He remained still—waiting.

She took a deep breath and then exhaled quickly. "The Sinclairs and Delaneys have been friends for more years than I have been alive. We've always been a part of each other's life."

"Do you want him?"

She blinked. "What?"

"I said. Do. You. Want. Him?"

"I don't understand what—"

"The hell you don't," he bellowed. "You were so wrapped up in that kiss you forgot I was in the motherfucking room. One thing I thought we had in this marriage was trust. But it seems we don't. We can end this farce right now."

Saying the words brought scathing heat to his chest. But he would be damned if he would hold on to a woman if she wanted to go, even though she was his wife.

"You're blowing this out of proportion. I won't be interrogated. Stop trying to put words into my mouth."

"You're trying to explain away the kiss." Disgust oozed through the words. "It won't work."

"You're stubborn and pig-headed. You get a notion in your mind or see something and assume the worse. Nothing can sway you. Everything isn't black or white, Jake."

"For me it is. You still didn't answer the question. Do you want your ex-husband back?"

She was silent for so long, he didn't think she would answer.

Melissa rubbed at her temples with the palms of her hands. "How can I? I'm married to you."

"That's no fucking answer," he shouted.

She charged at him, her feisty temper showing in her eyes. "Watch your mouth. I don't curse at you and I expect you to respect me and do the same."

Stung, he'd forgotten about her sharp tongue when she was cornered. He held back the coarse words he wanted to throw out. How in the hell had the tables turned such that she was angry with him? Her ire fueled his temper even more. He struggled not to lose it.

"I wasn't cursing at you," he ground out.

"The hell you weren't."

"Now, who's doing it?"

"Don't flip the chart, Jake. You won't win this."

"You're angry." He pinched the end of his nose and then ran a hand through his hair. "Unbelievable. You have the audacity to kiss another man—right in front me." His finger hit his chest. "I'm supposed to ignore or pretend it was nothing?"

"I didn't ask you to do that."

"Your actions spoke otherwise."

He wasn't a man who wasted time on regrets or mistakes; instead he opted to charge forward and tackle the situation—no matter how difficult. But right now he was in a fight for his marriage—his life. For the first time, he was afraid—he didn't want to know the answer but he wouldn't run from it.

"Do you want your ex-husband back?" he asked again.

The silence was deafening. It was long and dark. He was looking at her, but not really seeing her. Everything was, at that moment, bleak. A large weight was suspended in the air. It would eventually fall, and he couldn't decipher where it would land.

No sound came.

He waited.

And waited—no words were uttered.

Nothing.

Jake felt himself moving toward the door. The silence was suffocating. Escape—Escape. His mind screamed it over and over. He opened the door and walked out, leaving behind the hollow emptiness in the air. With the closing of the door, the weight finally found its resting spot.

CHAPTER THREE

For the hundredth time, Melissa looked at the clock on the wall. It was midnight and Jake still wasn't home. Where was he? She knew she'd made a mess of things and needed to make it right.

Brent had called to see if she was all right. She'd asked how he had gotten the number but he chuckled and said he knew people. In the old days, she would've laughed at his nonsense, but not now. She was concerned about Jake. Hell, she was worried Jake wouldn't come home tonight—or any other night. He was a prideful man with a large ego. Seeing his wife kiss another man and seemingly enjoying it must've been hard. Damn—she knew it was. How would she have felt if the situation was reversed? The thought caused great distress. But she and Jake didn't have a love marriage. He wanted a wife in his bed, one who eventually gave him children, but more importantly one who shared and understood his drive to continue the growth of his business. Ambition was Jake's middle name. It never bothered her that she wasn't his number one priority. She admired him but love—that was something she didn't do. She tried it once with Brent and came out of it with too many wounds and scars.

The garage door went up. Melissa stood waiting for him to throw his keys in the small ceramic basket on the table by the door, glance through the mail neatly stacked on the side counter and come down the hall to the great room. This was his ritual every day but tonight he didn't bother coming. He moved toward his office, went in and shut the door behind him.

Melissa moved slowly toward the office and stood in front of the door. Taking a cleansing breath, she opened the door and walked through.

He glanced at her over his shoulder and continued pouring scotch into a glass. With his back to her, he swallowed the contents and then filled it again. He took a sip and turned toward her.

"What do you want, Melissa?" His voice was gruff with agitation.

"We need to talk."

"Really? Now you want to talk. I asked you a question today. I'm finished talking. "

She entwined her fingers. "This is not easy for me, Jake. But I can't answer upon demand."

His laugh was hard. "Believe me sweetheart, you gave me your answer."

She frowned. "What is that, Jake?"

He slammed the glass on the table by the sofa. "I asked if you wanted him." He pointed to her. "You stiffened, pursed those damn pretty lips of yours, and tightened your stance. That leaves me to make an assumption that you want him. Am I right to do so or am I wrong?"

She opened her mouth and shut it. Jake was a master interrogator but she wouldn't be the target—not tonight. Granted, she was confused when it came to Brent. She'd loved him for a long time. It wasn't something that could be turned on and off like a light switch.

"Brent—"

"Don't. Speak. His. Name. Not in my presence. I'm not going to talk about him or the past you so conveniently kept silent." He drained the rest of the whiskey in his glass and placed it on the counter of the mini-bar. "I'm going to bed." He moved toward the door but stopped. "Don't worry. You can have the master suite all to yourself where you can dream about your ex-husband. I won't be a third party in my own bed. Not tonight. Not ever."

"How dare you say that to me!"

"I dare a damn lot, lady." He stalked to her. "I don't share."

"When we made love, I was with you all the way. I've never given you cause to believe I was thinking of another man."

He laughed. It was cruel and harsh, wrapping around her like steel bars. "We never made love. It was sex— or fucking. Take your pick."

She slapped him hard across his face, leaving an imprint. "Don't you ever speak to me like that again. What happened today in your office was impulse. It wasn't meant to hurt you or to belittle what we have. But you have too much pride to understand or listen to an explanation."

She'd never hit another human being in her life and she felt immediate remorse. He had a right to be angry— that she could deal with, but not his disrespect.

She bit her lip. The shock of what she did overwhelmed her. What was happening to her? "I'm sorry...I hit you. I've never done anything like that in my life. It was wrong," she said, trying to hold back the tears.

He pulled her roughly into his arms. Entwining his hands in her hair, he pulled her head back and captured the pulse beating in her neck with his tongue.

"So soft...smooth...beautiful," he groaned.

He suckled and then planted his mouth beside hers. She smelled the liquor on his breath, strong tobacco and a slight hint of a female's cologne. She reared back, almost stumbling in the process.

"Where have you been?"

"Does it matter?"

She stared at him, blinking back the tears. "Yes, it matters."

His laugh was harsh and angry. "Why?"

"We're married."

His twisted smile speared her heart. "Now you remember." He glared at her with such contempt she almost retreated from the room. "Married people are supposed to share—communicate and not tell each other lies."

"I never lied to you."

"Lady, you lied! Big time."

"I—"

"Lying by omission is still a lie."

"I can't talk to you when you're like this."

"The hell you won't."

"You're acting like a crazy man."

He threw out a sarcastic grunt. "If I am. You made me this way."

"You're drunk and smelling of cheap perfume."

"I'm not drunk." He started for the door but she moved, locked it and stood with her back against it. To get out, he would physically have to move her. She realized he never denied being with another woman. The realization of that fact hurt her more deeply than she thought possible.

"You're going to listen, whether you want to or not. I was born and raised in Dallas. My grandfather was white and my grandmother was a mixture of Sioux, Irish, and African-American. My mother was a product of their union. She married my father, a white man, the year she graduated from college. I came along three years later. To my mother's surprise, I wasn't what she expected."

"Why? She wanted a son?"

"No, I had brown skin. My mother was hoping for a pale child. One that didn't remind her of her black lineage. My mother was fair— almost fair enough to pass for white."

"That's ridiculous. That's not important any longer."

"My mother thought so."

"What about your father?"

"He loved me but he loved my mother more. Whatever she wanted, he gave it to her except the white child she wanted." She took a long, deep breath. "I found refuge at the Sinclair's. I spent all my free time with them.

"The Sinclair children consisted of Ashton, and twins, Brent and Gia. I became best friends with the twins but there was always a special bond between me and Brent. I didn't realize it was love until I turned sixteen. I began to see him differently. I knew my mother wanted a link between the families and when she found out how I felt about him, she encouraged it. She became my mother—a real mother." Tears rolled down her cheeks at the memories. "We went to social functions, horseback riding, and shopping together. It was wonderful. I became what she wanted. My mother finally loved me. I felt special.

"When Brent and I got married it was one of the happiest days of my life. I was the center of my parents' affection. I had the man I loved—only there was one problem—Brent was in love with his brother's wife."

"Is that why you're still here?" He sneered. "He doesn't want you?"

She rolled her eyes. "Ashton and his wife, Nicole loved each other deeply. Once I realized where Brent's heart was, I filed for divorce and left Dallas."

"Just like that—you left," he said, incredulously.

"Yes. I refused to be a pawn or stick my head in the sand to hide from the truth. Today was the first time I've seen him in five years."

"You still love him." It was a statement.

"Of course, I love him. He's family."

"Then let me rephrase the question. Are you *in love* with him?

"It's difficult to explain or to categorize Brent in my life."

"Answer the question."

The air was thick and charged with emotion. She wanted to give him the truth but the answer might not be what he wanted to hear. "I don't know."

The silence that clouded the room was heavy with agony—distrust—hurt. She felt it and she knew he did also. His face was a hard, cold mask. His eyes reflected so much disgust and pain she wanted to beg him to forgive her. But she couldn't. Nothing she did would erase the doubt she'd just uttered.

"Do you expect me to stick around until you decide?"

"I just need some time, Jake." She stretched her hands toward him, but they didn't touch. "I'm confused...but I know everything will work out. It must."

"Wishing it won't make it happen, Melissa."

"I know," she said, softly.

He stared at her for a very long time. The silence stretched. The only sound in the room was the chime on the wall clock, announcing another hour had passed. She held his gaze, hoping he'd allow her to see some emotion, but he didn't. What was he thinking or feeling? Only the heightened color in his face displayed his anger at her admission.

"I'll take one of the guest bedrooms."

The thread of steel in his tone sounded so final. It sent an uncomfortable feeling through her. She was scared.

"What's that going to solve?" she said, urgently.

"We need space. We put the cart before the horse and now we're paying for it, or rather I am."

They both were like two bulls in a stand-off. She moved from the door, he opened it and walked through without looking back.

She blinked back the tears that flooded her eyes. Her heart was beating erratically, threatening to steal air from her lungs. She choked on her sobs. Finally, she knew what she'd always known—she didn't want to lose him.

CHAPTER FOUR

Sheila's mouth moved but Melissa couldn't hear a thing. Her mind kept drifting back to the conversation she had with Jake.

For the first time in her life, she'd talked about her parents and the misery of growing up in a home devoid of parental love. Jake had mostly remained silent. After she was finished, he then walked out. That was three days ago. Each night he came home well past midnight and was gone by the time she arrived in the kitchen at 6 a.m. She took a sip of diet soda, glanced around the busy restaurant to gather her thoughts and leaned back against the cushioned seat.

"You haven't heard a word I've said." Sheila's tone was laced with a little irritation. "What's wrong with you?"

She tucked her hair behind her ear while she struggled to remember what Sheila was talking about. "I'm sorry, my mind was drifting. What did you say?"

Her friend tilted her head.

Melissa gently rubbed her tired eyes. Surviving on four hours of sleep per night was taking its toll.

She sighed and looked at her friend. "Alright. Let me have it."

"I have known you for almost five years. I believe I know when something is wrong."

"I'm fine. I just have a lot on my mind." She pointed at Sheila's round, pregnant belly. "How are you feeling? Excited yet? Does John want another boy or girl? John Jr. is four now. Is he looking forward to being a big brother?"

"Wow."

"What?"

"You're really stressed. You never talk or ask questions in rapid succession. So come on and give. Is it Jake? He's my cousin but I'll always have your back. I know Jake can be a bear. What has he done?"

Melissa squirmed in her seat. She wasn't discussing Jake with Sheila. Although, she was her best friend long before she married Jake, Sheila was his family. To make matters more uncomfortable, the both of them were thick as thieves. That changed the parameters as to what were acceptable topics of conversation.

Sheila Sorenson-Flaherty, a beautiful, smart and petite blonde, was one of the best prosecutors in the state of California until she decided to get married and have babies. Being a stay-at-home mom agreed with her. It also helped that was she married to renowned entertainment attorney, John Flaherty. A tall Irishman, with jet-black hair and piercing dark eyes, he looked more like a dashing movie star than a lawyer. Sheila and he complemented each other in looks and personality.

She could intercept bullshit. Not much got past her.

"Nothing. I just have a lot on my mind. We've been courting James Lakeland for a few months now. It looks as if he's ready to sell but he's being skittish. I don't want to blow this deal."

"Are you kidding me? You're one of the best negotiators at Sorensen Group. I have never known you to be nervous about a merger or a sale."

Melissa grabbed her glass and drank deeply. "There's a first time for everything."

Sheila was silent for a long moment. Her deep gray eyes, so like her cousin's, stared holes into her armor. "I know it's more than that, so give."

"I saw my ex-husband for the first time in years."

"Oh, my goodness. Is he here...in L.A?"

"Yes." She was quiet for a moment. "Jake knows about my previous marriage."

"I told you to tell him before the two of you got married."

Sheila had found out she was married during one of their tipsy girl's getaway weekends. Melissa had talked too much about her past and woke up with a tremendous hangover the next morning. She hadn't realized how much of her life she'd exposed until her friend mentioned it. Sheila had admonished her to tell Jake. She scoffed at the idea. At the time Jake was just someone she was dating and didn't expect it to develop into anything serious. She'd asked Sheila not to say anything about her previous marriage to him. Although she hadn't liked it, Sheila kept her secret.

"I know what you said. I just didn't think it was important. His proposal was non-traditional. He laid out the facts why he thought we should get married and I agreed. There was none of the flowery stuff or getting down on one knee. To be honest, his proposal came as a surprise. I never envisioned him as the marrying type but we do work well together."

Sheila laughed. "I know you're not that blind. Jake is a tough man. Some would say downright dangerous. His company is extremely successful and he has more money than he would ever spend. He makes no allowances for his business or his personal life. He married you because he wanted you."

"Our marriage isn't based on a fairytale," Melissa insisted.

"You're sleeping with the man but you don't know him at all."

Melissa sucked her teeth and frowned deeply. "Okay. Since I don't know anything about my husband, why don't you tell me?"

"Nope." Sheila tipped her mineral water to her lips and sipped." This is one you have to work out yourself. Let me give you a little advice. Your ex-husband is your past. Leave him there."

"Brent and I have been over for a long time."

"Really? It may be for him, but what about you?"

Melissa lowered her eyes and then looked at her friend. "It's done...history." Her heart pounded at the words, knowing there was unfinished business with her ex-husband. She just didn't know how much. But she knew if she let it prolong, it could cost her Jake.

"Good. How did the two of you reconnect anyway?"

"Brent was in Jake's office when I walked in a few days ago."

"Wow. Are you kidding me? Was he looking for you?"

"No. He was there on business."

Sheila's eyes widened. "Damn. Jake must've felt like a fool when he realized the man he was meeting was your ex-husband."

"I didn't know who he was until he turned around." Melissa said defensively. "I was shocked and so was he. I hadn't seen him since I left Dallas five years ago. It's what happened next that caused the rift with Jake."

"Don't tell me you locked lips with the man," she joked.

Melissa clasped her fingers tightly in her lap and tried to appear calm. Sheila's eyes were glued on her.

"It happened before I knew it. I didn't stop to think about how it may have looked to Jake. It was as if time stood still and waited for Brent and me to catch up."

"I was *only*..." Sheila fell back in her chair, her mouth gaped open. "You mean to tell me Jake witnessed the lip-fest reunion? Did you explain the kiss meant nothing?"

"No."

"What do you mean no?"

"I couldn't honestly say it was nothing. Although we got divorced, I have loved him for a long time. He occupied a large part of my heart. It's been that way most of my life."

Her friend looked at her as if she'd lost her mind. "Damn. Melissa. The man dumped you for another woman and you're still hung up on him?"

"It's a lot more complicated than that. We have history."

"Tell Jake that and see what happens." Sheila paused for a moment. "Are you leaving my cousin for your ex?"

She said it with such reproach that Melissa was taken aback. The thought never crossed her mind. Thinking about it now left heaviness in her chest she couldn't decipher. She knew the path she was going down could cause a lot of problems but she needed to examine what was happening between her and Brent. She owed it to herself. Didn't she?

"Couples run into rough patches, Sheila."

"You've only been married for three months."

"We'll get through it," she said, forcefully.

"You won't with your ex still in the picture."

"Jake is just being stubborn. He'll come around."

It came out with more confidence than she felt.

"Go ahead and keep the blinders on, my friend. Jake isn't going to sit back and wait for you to get another man out of your system. Life doesn't work that way, especially with a Sorensen."

"I'll figure it out."

"Is your ex-husband still in town?"

"I believe so."

"Have you met with him?"

"No."

Sheila's laser gaze held hers. "But you're in contact with him," she said matter-of-factly.

"We've talked on the phone. The scene in Jake's office wasn't pretty. He wanted to make sure I was alright."

The excuse sounded flimsy even to her ears.

"You want to see him again, don't you?"

Melissa frowned. "I'm not on trial, Sheila."

"Then you have nothing to hide, do you?"

She was silent.

"You don't have to say anything. I see it in your eyes." Sheila grunted, disgust was evident in her tone. "You're my friend, but Jake is my blood. He's rough around the edges, but still a great man. He doesn't let down his guard easily, but he did with you. A lot of people see him as cold and heartless but there's a side of him that's vulnerable, especially when it comes to you. I won't stand idly by and see him hurt."

"I have no intention of hurting him."

"You already have."

Melissa flinched. "This isn't about Jake, it's about my demons and I need to exorcise them. I thought I had gotten past the betrayal I felt when Brent told me he wanted out of the marriage. I didn't believe I would recover. I felt helpless and inadequate. He was in love with another woman. How did I compete? I kept asking myself, what did she have that I didn't? Maybe if I'd lost more weight he would want me. What did she do for him that I didn't do?

Melissa was breathing hard. She fought to hold back the tears as bile rose in her throat. She swallowed a few times to grab hold of her runaway emotions. Rehashing that time in her life hurt as much as it did all those years ago.

Sheila laid her hand on top of hers. "I'm sorry, Melissa. I can't begin to know how you must've felt. But it doesn't excuse what you're doing now. Life has given you a second chance. You are a grown woman and married to a wonderful man. He's not perfect but he's loyal. Of course, he has his faults. Who doesn't? But he's a decent and honorable person. Don't let your past ruin your future."

Melissa removed her hand and put it in her lap to stop the trembling.

"I won't," she uttered, half-heartedly. She felt embarrassed at how much she'd revealed.

After a long moment of silence, Sheila said, "You're heading down a dark road, Melissa. But I'm not going to continue to press the issue. I would like to ask, did you know the woman?"

Melissa nodded. "She was a part of our group of friends. We all hung out together. Her aunt and Brent's mother were best friends. I could tell she had a crush on Brent. It didn't matter because all the girls did. I ignored it. We were so young and carefree back then. I always thought of her as his little sister because that was how he treated her. But things changed. I didn't know about his feelings for her until after we were married. I was devastated but I was determined to hold on to him."

"You're still holding on to him."

Melissa took a deep breath. "Brent and I need closure."

"Really? It sounds like it's much more. Maybe you want to see if the fire is still burning. You're fooling yourself and playing a dangerous game, Melissa. Jake won't let you belittle or shame him. You need to respect what you have with Jake. You'd better be careful. Being alone is a bitch."

"You don't understand."

"You're right and I don't want to."

"I've got to go." Sheila placed bills on the table, and walked through the restaurant doors.

Melissa was afraid she might have lost her best friend—her only friend.

CHAPTER FIVE

"I want to see you—I need to see you."

Melissa pressed the phone to her ear. Brent's words resonated in her ears, warmed her body, and caused her heart to beat unbelievably fast.

The morning wasn't starting off the way she wanted. Sleep had eluded her most of the night while she waited for Jake to come home. She'd dozed off around 2 a.m. She woke an hour later, went to the guest room where Jake now resided and knocked on the bedroom door. When there was no answer, she opened the door. The bed was neatly made and showed no evidence of occupation. She searched the entire house before she realized he wasn't there.

Hurt and wondering where he could be, Melissa laid awake listening for his footsteps on the hardwood floors but they never came.

Jake hadn't come home last night— again. Everything was crumbling around her and she was letting it. She shook her head to clear her troubled mind.

"I'm surprised you're still in Los Angeles, Brent. I thought you had left."

"I'll be in town a couple more days."

"It's been over a week. Why are you still here?"

"I had other business to attend to. Besides, I still needed to meet with Sorensen again on the deal I proposed to him."

Surprised, Melissa swallowed and cleared her throat. "You met with Jake?"

"Yes. Two days ago. You didn't know?"

She didn't answer his question but asked one of her own.

"What happened with the proposal?"

"It was a good one and he knew it. I must say I was surprised. I thought for sure he would allow his personal feelings to squash the deal."

"Well, you don't know Jake. He doesn't let emotion interfere with business." Her tone was harsh, which was a surprise. Jake was a businessman first, everything else came in second. It never bothered her before and she didn't know why she had a problem with it now.

"Do I detect sarcasm?"

"No, I was only stating a fact."

"Have dinner with me," Brent said, abruptly.

She mulled over the invitation. Jake and she were married but strangers living under the same roof. At the office, she'd made an attempt to see him but his secretary had been given strict orders to not disturb him. Even his wife was listed on the do not disturb list. Angry and embarrassed, she hadn't tried to contact him again.

Jake didn't play games. When he was angry he came out fighting. The cut was direct and could be brutal. She hadn't seen him in almost two weeks. When she was at the house he made sure he wasn't. He came home well after the time when she was asleep. Some nights she tried to force herself to stay awake until she heard his footsteps, but she could never manage to do it.

"It's not necessary for us to have dinner. You can say what you need to now."

"No, I can't. A lot happened between us five years ago."

"It was a long time ago, Brent. I was a different person then. I'm over it."

The lie felt heavy on her tongue.

The silence stretched. She knew Brent, probably, more than he knew himself. He never liked having a heavy conscience. For him, everything needed to be neat and tidy. He wanted to make peace for his bad treatment but she didn't know if she was ready for it. Loving him had been one-sided. But she'd held on to hope that Brent would come to realize his feelings for Nicole were futile.

From the magazine articles and pictures she viewed, his brother, Ashton and Nicole seemed very happy with their two sons.

"Melissa, what are you afraid of?"

"Nothing."

"Then meet me for dinner."

She sighed. "Okay. Where?"

"My hotel."

"Excuse me?"

"Look, I have meetings all day and won't be finished until around seven. It would be easier for us to eat at the hotel."

"Alright," she said, feeling uncomfortable but ignoring it. "I'll be there around seven-thirty."

"Great. I'll meet you in the lobby."

"Good-bye, Brent."

Troubled, she severed the connection. Why did she agree to dinner? Melissa felt she was making a mistake—a big mistake but she couldn't seem to stop herself.

Jake sipped the bourbon in his glass and leaned back in the seat. "I'm glad we could meet, Mr. Lakeland."

The older man with thinning silver hair and a protruded stomach swallowed his gin and tonic. Raising his glass, he beckoned to the hovering waiter for a refill. Jake watched him with hooded eyes. Even though the man was reported to be a heavy drinker, he could hold his liquor and still be a tough negotiator.

Samuel Lakeland took the drink from the waiter. "I just finished a round of golf and dinner at my club. I was on my way home when I decided to give you a call. It was last minute but I hope you don't mind."

"No problem at all," Jake said. "I was glad to hear from you."

"Good. I've always liked the Beverly Wilshire."

"Yes. It's a nice hotel."

Jake casually scanned the people coming and going. Since it was a weeknight with no conventions in the hotel, the lobby wasn't crowded. He sipped the brown liquor again, hoping it would create numbness so he wouldn't think about his personal life. He settled comfortably in his chair to listen to his client.

A tall blond-haired man stood alone in the middle of the lobby looking at the front doors. From the back he seemed familiar, when he straightened and turned slightly toward him, Jake realized it was Brent Sinclair. What was he still doing in town? It wasn't long before a petite, curvy woman with thick brown hair pulled from her face into a high ponytail, entered the lobby heading for Sinclair.

"What the fu—" Jake squeezed his glass.

It was his wife.

She walked up to Brent. He wrapped his arms around her, planted a kiss on her cheek, and then quickly touched her lips to his. Melissa didn't pull away. She lingered in his embrace as if she

31

belonged there.

Sinclair was now talking. He smiled at her. She seemed to be in awe, not saying a word. Jake's temper rose with increased proportion as they continued to stand there with each other. Brent stepped back. Then he stretched out his right hand, she seemed to give a slight hesitation. He continued holding out his hand, giving her a choice.

Don't! —No sound—It only resonated in his mind.

His wife placed her hand in Brent's.

They walked the short distance to the elevator doors. He pushed the button but held her hand with his other.

Jake stood abruptly, moving quickly toward them.

"Mr. Sorensen—"

He heard his client but didn't react. He had almost reached the elevator when the doors opened and Melissa and Brent got on.

Fear screamed through his body.

The ringing in his ears caused him to stumble.

He kept moving.

The door closed in his face.

Closing them in.

Shutting him out.

CHAPTER SIX

Brent swung open the door to his hotel room and stepped back. Melissa dropped her head contemplating if she should enter. Her heart was beating fast. She didn't belong here. "Turn around and go home," she told herself. She didn't.

"Melissa, what's wrong?" he asked.

The contour of his voice wrapped her in its warmth. She lifted her head and their eyes connected. His eyes, the color of the Caribbean waters, clear and blue filled with something she couldn't explain searched hers. Her gaze roamed his, wondering how they had come to this place. She admitted to herself she'd missed him in the last five years with an ache that scarred her for any other man—even Jake. She bit her lip. That wasn't true. No man compared to Jake. He was an enigma all by himself: strong, dominant and the best lover she ever had. At first they were employer and employee, then involved sexually, but not romantically. Sometimes she didn't understand their relationship but it worked for them. It was easy, comfortable and passionate.

However, the experience with Brent had left her cautious and vowing never to become vulnerable again. Many times she watched confusion on Jake's face when she would put up the wall between them. But it didn't stop her from doing it. It was a safety mechanism she learned during the last days of her marriage to Brent.

"Melissa, this is only dinner," he said, hurriedly.

"I know." She stepped over the threshold, immediately noticing the earth tones and simplistic design features of the luxury suite. Melissa turned toward him. "The room is nice." She set her purse on the high table by the door. The latch on the door snapped behind her. She stiffen at the sound, closing her inside the room, becoming instantly nervous.

He stood at her back, his body enveloping her, as he leaned his head on her shoulder.

She tried not to react to his nearness. He'd done this many times when they were teenagers. It meant nothing.

"We don't need to make small talk," he said against her ear. "Conversation always flowed easily between us. Come."

He moved and led her by the hand to the round table in the middle of the room. It was beautifully prepared with candles, a tiered centerpiece of red and yellow roses, and place settings of fine china and gold silverware. A cart stood by the table laden with dishes covered with silver domes. It looked too romantic and made her a little uncomfortable. She coughed slightly to clear the sudden thump in her throat.

"You alright?" Brent's blue gaze looked at her with concern.

"I'm fine."

He released her hand, pulled out a chair and directed her to sit. He moved to the other seat and sat, reaching to uncover the dishes.

"I had the chef prepare all your favorites, grilled shrimp and fresh crab meat swimming in lemon butter sauce, lobster garlic mashed potatoes and steamed asparagus sprinkled with fresh basil and scallions."

"Wow."

He laughed. "I remember how you liked to lick the sauce off of your fingers."

"My mother hated when I did that."

"I know. Your mother is definitely a character—a refined one— but definitely a character."

She offered a small smile. "I believe she would've found that to be a compliment."

She bit into the seafood mixture and then delicately licked the sauce that escaped at the corner of her mouth. Taking the crisp, cloth napkin, she dabbed her lips and then wiped her hands.

"Yummy. I'm impressed."

"I didn't do it to impress you."

She ate some of the asparagus and then more shrimp and crab. "Really? Then why? You never did this when we were married."

"I made a mistake, Melissa."

"Are you apologizing?"

"Profusely."

"No need. There's no flood. The water is under the bridge."

"You always had a way with words."

She drank the ice water in the stemmed glass. "I try."

"You deserve to be treated like royalty."

"Since when?" Her tone was sarcastic, but she didn't care at the moment.

He shot her a tight, sad smile. "You have a right to be angry."

"I'm not angry—just disappointed." She leaned back in the chair and glared at him. "You were my friend, who hurt me—deeply."

"I know. I didn't realize how much until this moment. I didn't treat you right. Call it being young, careless of your feelings and thinking the world was mine to do what I wanted."

"Women were always at your disposal." She drank more of the water, loving the coldness as it glided down her throat.

Brent didn't say anything for the briefest moment and then he nodded. "You're right. Women were never a problem. I never lied to you about that."

"I thought it would be different when we got married."

"Being cocky, I didn't think it mattered."

"It mattered." She swallowed and said again," It mattered a great deal to me."

"I know." The words were spoken with regret.

Nothing more was spoken while they ate.

"You didn't touch the potatoes." He pointed to the smooth mound on her plate.

She dipped her fork in the creamy mixture filled with chunks of lobster. She chewed and savored the flavors. He was right, they were heavenly.

"They're very rich and fattening." Melissa tried to stifle a moan of pleasure.

"I'm glad you like them. I tried to give the chef the precise instructions. I hope I got them right. Besides, you could stand to gain a few pounds."

"Shh...Don't ever say that in front of my mother," she joked. "She always watched her weight, and mine too."

He laughed, leaned back in his chair and watched her. It made her very uneasy. So she glanced around the room. The lights were dimmed. Soft music played through the ceiling speakers. It was too romantic and it made her nervous. She was quite aware of him...the good times they'd shared...this wasn't good. Not at all.

"The meal was delicious. Thank you, but I'm full."

She pushed away from the table, stood and walked to the

fireplace. It was rude to do so, but she needed to create distance between them. She couldn't pretend any longer they were friends having a casual dinner.

He came and stood in front of her. His eyes locked on her, traveling to her lips. He leaned forward and planted a soft kiss on her mouth. A hint of butter and lemon lingered. She fought not to lick her lips and savor the taste.

"Why did you do that?"

Warmth and a tingling sensation cruised through her body.

He shrugged. "I'm sorry. I didn't intend for it to make you uncomfortable."

"It didn't." She lied.

He smiled. "Good."

Why did he kiss her? Did she really want to know? She had no answer.

"You went through a lot of trouble getting the chef to prepare this meal. Chinese or Pizza would have been fine."

"Aww. Your favorite unhealthy foods."

"You remembered."

"I did. But I felt you deserved better tonight."

It was unsettling, after all this time apart, he could still gage her mood. So could Jake, she thought. He was a master at it. She wouldn't think about him tonight. It was odd being here with Brent but she was determined to focus on what was happening presently.

Silence fell between them.

"Talk to me, Melissa. We used to share so much."

"That was a long time ago."

"Time is not a factor. We have tonight." His grin was boyish and charming.

Her heart flipped in her chest. She shouldn't be here. Then he wrapped his arms around her, leaned in for another kiss, and she let him. It was pleasant and comforting.

"I've known you all my life. That must count for something," he said.

Melissa moved from his warm embrace, creating much needed space, and folded her arms. "What do you want from me, Brent?"

He laughed. "How about a glass of wine? We never touched it." He lifted the bottle out of the ice bucket and poured the Veramonte Sauvignon Blanc into the empty glasses on the table. He handed one to her. She sipped, enjoying the bold and rich flavor against her tongue.

"How did you find this wine? It's nearly impossible to get."

"I know. It comes from the Argentine and Chilean highlands. Fortunately for us, the hotel stocks a bottle or two in their cellar."

"Nice."

"I'm glad you like it."

He took her hand and led her to the sofa. They sat beside each other—almost touching. It was very intimate. Between the music and wine, she felt warm and giddy.

She cleared her throat. "Do you live in Chicago now?"

"For the past two years. But I also lived in Hong Kong for a year and then another year in Spain."

"Why?"

"The family company has expanded all over the globe. I have spearheaded those new ventures."

"Ah, I see. You have become a vagabond."

He shifted in his seat. "I wouldn't say that. I was needed, so I went."

She stared at him for a moment. "You were running away. Why won't you go home to Dallas?"

"It's complicated."

She set the glass on the end table beside her, and took a deep breath. "You're still in love with Nicole."

He gulped the last of his wine. "Why do you say that?"

"Because I know how much you love your family. Nothing would keep you away unless it was too painful to be with them."

"You know what happened between Ashton and me. It's easier if I keep my distance."

"But—"

"Stop." Brent put his glass on the table, inched closer to her on the sofa. Their knees touched and his hand cupped her cheek. "I didn't invite you here tonight to talk about my family. This is a second chance for us. I've made a lot of mistakes. Some I can't correct but I would like to try."

"You can begin with your brother. Ashton would forgive you for anything, you know that."

He laughed harshly. "I don't think any man could forget or forgive another man for trying to steal his wife."

"Have you tried to mend your relationship?"

He nodded. "We consciously co-exist."

"What does that mean?"

"I travel a lot. Ashton is based in the Dallas office. We gather at the parents' house for Thanksgiving and Christmas but other than that, we stay out each other's way. I can pretend for two days out of the year that my brother and I don't hate each other's guts."

"You can't mean that. Ashton isn't the sort of man to hold grudges. He loves you."

"You sound like Nicole."

Surprised, she stopped speaking for a moment.

"You still talk to Nicole?"

"Only in Ashton's presence," he said sarcastically.

"I see."

"I don't think you do. Nicole is a peacemaker. She wants to bring Ashton and me together." He sighed. "Maybe one day we'll be able to sit and talk together without animosity."

"That's ridiculous. Ashton didn't steal Nicole from you."

"I know. But it's still hard to swallow that he has her love."

Old hurts rose to the forefront again but she pushed through them.

"She's not yours, Brent. Never will be. It's time you let her go," she said stressed.

"You're right." He ran a hand through his blonde locks, causing them to spike. "Forgive me. I'm being insensitive."

"I've recovered from the stumbling blocks in my past. Although there was a time I didn't think I would. I had such low self-esteem. I made you my world."

"I realize that now." He stared hard at her. "I had forgotten how beautiful you are."

His words caught her by surprise. Immediately she was uncomfortable, her breath caught in her throat.

Brent's hands went to her hair pulling it from the neat ponytail she'd constructed.

"So beautiful," he murmured again.

His lips grazed hers and then his tongue parted her slightly opened lips. She felt hers slide against his. He deepened the kiss, she gasped at the warm sensation cruising through her body, but her mind rebelled.

She pushed at his shoulders. "Stop."

His beautiful blue eyes penetrated through her.

"This is wrong, Brent."

He rested his forehead on hers. "Damn, Melissa." A sigh resignation escaped. "I'm sorry. Sex has always been easy for us...and good."

"But it's only brought us confusion and trouble."

He raked a hand through his messy hair again, scrubbed his face and gnawed on this bottom lip.

"You can't deny you responded to the kiss."

'Neither one of us want this."

"How can you say that? The chemistry is still there. You're hurting. I'm hurting. Why not give each other comfort."

"We went down that road the last weeks of our marriage. I almost got destroyed in the process."

"I'm sorry. I should not have said that."

"You're right." She grimaced. "Seeing you again conjured up memories. It would be easy to submit to the familiar. It's comfortable but wrong for both of us. I apologize. I sent you mixed signals. I would never cheat on my husband."

"He means that much to you?"

"Yes."

"I screwed up again, didn't I?"

Her eyes quickly met his before turning back to stare at the flames in the fireplace. It was October and today was unusually cool in Los Angeles. Even though the room was comfortable, she wrapped her arms around her waist to ward off a sudden chill.

They both stood and moved the marble fireplace. "Let's discuss why I'm here."

He pinched the end of his nose and then took a deep breath. He started to pace with agitated quick movements. "I took you for granted. Hell. I apologize—"

"Stop saying you're sorry." She stared at him, tension swirling in her gut. She swallowed. "Hell, with my state of mind, I *needed* for you to love me."

"I did love you. You were one of my best friends."

"From the time we were teenagers, I always wanted more." She shrugged and then let out a weary breath. "I guess that was my life's mission to always want more than I could have. My parents' love—and then yours. I made some bad choices but I take responsibility for them."

"Is Jake Sorensen one of those bad choices?"

She flinched as if he'd struck her. "Jake has nothing to do with this."

"Doesn't he? If you weren't on the outs with your husband, would you be here in my hotel room? Would you have accepted my kisses?"

"You still can be a son-of-bitch, Brent."

"I'm sorry...Please forgive me." He wrapped his arms around her. "When it comes to you, I'm protective. You still hold a special place in my heart. That will never change."

"But it was never enough for us." She eased out of his arms. "I don't want your pity. I had enough of that. It's taken me years to finally like myself—just the way I am. I won't lose my hard earned self-esteem. I'm stronger and smarter than I was five years ago. I have grown a lot. I don't crave people's acceptance any longer. I complete myself."

"You're different. This Melissa I don't know, but I like her. You're confident—more assertive with your words." He was quiet for a moment. "The parents wanted the marriage. Hell, they expected it."

Melissa allowed his words to penetrate into the recesses of her mind. She felt the pain of their divorce, of being discarded, but there was comfort in the fact that for the first time in their relationship they were talking—really talking. Unfortunately, she and Brent had ended their marriage in cold silence.

"I wanted my mother's approval and love so badly; I probably would've done anything to get it. Being here tonight...with you...helped me to find answers."

His look was quizzical.

"Everything between us was temporal. It should've never happened," she said.

"For a while, it was good with us. We were compatible where it mattered."

She shook her head. "Sex won't hold a marriage together,

Brent."

He produced his winning smile. "I don't see why not. Even during the bad times, the sex was off the hook...*damn good*."

"You're unbelievable. We're not discussing our past sex life."

"Too late. I already did."

"Brent, be serious."

"Alright. Let's finish this. If you want to know if I was *in love* with you..." He stared at her for a long moment. "Back then, I didn't know what it felt like to be in love. Hell, all I wanted was to get laid—as many times as I could."

She cringed at his bluntness.

As if to soften the blow, he drew her closer to his chest. She tried not to focus on the strong, steady beat of his heart, and the power she felt beneath her fingers.

"I was your *best friend* before Nicole moved to Dallas. Then everything changed," she said, missing the bond they once shared.

Brent frowned. "You were jealous of Nicole?"

"I wasn't jealous—well, not at first. As time passed, I realized she was in love with you." She shrugged. "You didn't notice how she felt, so I ignored it. By then we were having a sexual relationship and I presumed we were an item."

"I thought you would always be around—no matter what I did. I was an arrogant ass. I never wanted to get married but never voiced it to anyone...not even myself. When I finally did, it was too late, we were already married."

Shocked, she uttered, "You knew the marriage was a mistake before you realized your feelings for Nicole?"

"Yeah. Remember you and your mother talked about a big wedding?"

She nodded.

"Well, I got stinking drunk to drown out the word wedding."

"Is that why you talked me into eloping?"

"I thought once it was done, the panic I was experiencing would disappear. Hell, I couldn't understand it. I liked you. You were gorgeous, smart and great in bed. What more could a man ask for?" He threw her a crooked grin.

"I wished you had told me about your doubts."

"I know. People were hurt, your parents, mine, but you received the brunt of it."

"And Nicole?"

"Ah, yes." He sighed, softly. "Nicole. The night of my parents' anniversary party and our wedding reception, she told me she loved me. It came as a shock but I felt something I had never felt before." He paused. "It was too late for us. I was married to you. By the time I realized I wanted to explore a relationship with Nicole, she had turned to Ashton. She eventually fell in love with him." For a moment he was silent. "I hate to admit it but they are made for each other. The end."

"Where does that leave you, Brent?"

A sad smile shot across his face. "Moving on with my life."

"I hope so."

He sighed. "A few months after you left Dallas, I hired a private investigator to find you."

"Really? Why?"

"I knew I had hurt you. I needed to know you were safe. He found you living in Nevada. After I received the report, I told him to drop it. Seeing you in Sorensen's office was a shock."

"For me also. Where do we go from here, Brent?"

"Friends?"

"I don't believe so...or at least not like before."

"Why? Because of Sorensen?"

"Partly."

"And what else?"

"We have lost too much. There's been too much pain between

us. We can't turn back the hands on the clock. But you still have a chance to rebuild your relationship with your brother. You need to let Nicole go. She'll never be yours."

Saying those words made her feel better but also freed her. She wasn't a vindictive person. But knowing that Brent didn't end up with everything he wanted gave her a measure of peace. Some decisions you make have life altering consequences.

"Like I said, I've accepted it and moved on."

"Who are you trying to convince, me or yourself?"

His eyes narrowed. "Your fangs are showing, Melissa."

"No, Brent. It's the truth. No matter how much it hurts, you have to own yours."

"I don't need a philosophy lesson."

"I'm not giving one."

"Enough. Why did you leave Nevada?"

"I never intended to stay. It was a stopover of sorts. A place to get my head together."

He grinned. "Such a pretty head." He paused for a moment; his beautiful eyes scanned her face and finally rested on her lips. "You're still a lovely...enchanting woman..." As if lost in thought, he rubbed his fingers across her skin. "Smooth ...Creamy...Melissa?"

His tone was soft; creating warmth she knew could be dangerous. But his tense gaze unnerved her. She couldn't read what was going on in his brain. She sensed a hidden message in the words and felt a prickle of discomfort. She shook her head slightly to rid herself of the sensation.

"Don't. Brent."

His eyes widened, and then his lips tilted into a half grin.

"What?"

"Not going to happen."

"The chemistry—"

"Please don't."

"Alright. But the connection we have can't be denied."

She wouldn't entertain it with a response. Besides, in her vulnerable state she didn't know where it would lead. She realized going down memory lane was dangerous—just too dangerous.

He cleared his throat. "In all the years apart, I never thought for a moment you would re-marry."

"Really? Did you think you may have scarred me for life?" Her laugh was brittle.

"I thought your hatred of me would've stopped you from trusting another man again."

It almost did but she wouldn't tell him that.

"I did question my ability to believe in what I was feeling. But, I could never hate you, Brent."

"I'm glad. Sorensen—is he worthy of you? If not, I'll do everything in my power to make sure he is."

"What are you going to do, beat him into submission?"

"If I have to."

The words came out harsh and cold. It surprised her. Melissa frowned at him.

"That's your ego talking."

"My ego?" He seemed surprise at her statement. "I always tried to protect you."

"But you couldn't protect me from you."

He flinched. "You're right," he said, softly. "My mistake."

She looked at him long and hard. She could finally let him go— in her heart and mean every word of it. Seeing him again, helped to realize they should've never crossed the friendship line.

Crossing the intimate boundary was a huge mistake. It could never be rectified. In her desperate need to be loved and to belong to someone, she had given him her virginity. She didn't regret it. He had been gentle and taught her about passion. But the desire to create a family of her own clouded her judgment when it came to him.

But it had been different with Jake. The first time she met him, she'd been immediately drawn and aware of his powerful and masculine aura. The attraction between them was fast and consuming to the point it had frightened her at first. She'd never felt like that with Brent. With him her attraction had been easy—comfortable. Jake was a storm—fire—and lightning.

Her husband took her breath away. For the first time, she examined her feelings for Jake. She missed him. His gruffness—his brooding stares—his inability to tolerate bullshit, and take no prisoners attitude. He could arouse her with just a look, a fleeting touch or kiss. He was direct, but she loved that about him. Her breath caught in her throat. Love? Where did that come from? She didn't love Jake. She couldn't—she wouldn't. But she did. She wanted Jake any way she could have him.

There was nothing in this hotel room for her. Closure for her was the day she walked out of Brent's house and filed for divorce. She never looked back.

"I've got to go, Brent."

"Now?" He frowned. "But we haven't finished talking."

"Yes, we have."

He was silent for a long moment, staring at her with confusion and then with understanding of who they were now.

"This is the end, isn't it?"

She nodded. Relief and a peace she never experienced before settled over her.

"It took me seeing you again to realize I was holding on to a dream and not reality. Our friendship was real but the other—it wasn't. A long time ago you filled a void. We were lazily swimming with the waves and not with each other." She laughed at the realization of it all. "I'm good, Brent. Really good. I forgive you for everything, but more importantly, I forgive myself."

She took a deep cleansing breath, enjoying the freshness of it. She lightly touched his cheek.

"Thank you for taking care of a lonely and shy girl for all those years. Our marriage was an unstable foundation from the beginning. It was doomed to fail."

"Melissa—"

"It's our truth, Brent." She smiled. "It doesn't hurt anymore."

"Little Melissa Delaney has grown up."

"Thank you for everything."

Melissa gave him a tight hug. He returned it. She stepped away, picked up her purse from the table and placed her hand on the doorknob. She turned and studied him. Brent stood in the middle of the room in a relaxed stance, with his head tilted, staring at her.

He looked the same as he did five years earlier. He carried a slight tan, which didn't surprise her. Brent loved the outdoors. His blond hair lay smooth against his head and cut neatly around his ears. He was tall with an athletic six-one build. Time had been good to him. Nothing changed. At least not for him. But a whole new world had opened for her.

He threw her that beautiful smile he was known for, his smoldering, blue eyes connecting with hers. She waited for her heart to do a frenzied palpitation—it didn't. A sure sign that it was over for her.

"Brent, someday, you'll meet the right woman and when it happens, it'll change your entire life. Be happy, Brent."

She opened the door and walked out.

❧

In the dark, Jake sat in the large sofa chair near the bar, sipped his third glass of scotch, and watched the front door. It was well past midnight. He wasn't tired but neither was he drunk. One thing was for sure, he was mad as hell. Anger burned in his gut like bitter gall.

This wasn't how he imagined his life with Melissa, she with another man and he consumed with disgust and pain. Damn. He wasn't willing to let her go, no matter the circumstances. He still loved her. The very first time he saw her, he fell hard. After his experience with his girlfriend, he never thought he would open himself to another woman. They could be manipulative, cunning and deceitful. He didn't want to fall in love. Love caused a person to lose control. Something he didn't relish doing. But when Melissa had turned her deep, smoldering dark eyes on him. He was lost from that moment on.

His former flame had left him twelve years ago to become a runway model. The bright light of fame was a powerful magnet he couldn't fight. To be honest, he was glad he escaped while he had the chance. Today the woman had achieved the fame she sought. However, along with living the high-life came five divorces attached to her name.

The front door opened quietly and the petite silhouette of his wife stepped over the threshold, shutting the door with hurried movement. She reached for the light switch but he clicked the button on the lamp sitting on the end table beside him. She gasped, a slim hand going to her throat.

"Jake. You scared me." She moved further into the room. "When did you get home?"

He didn't say anything but continued to watch her progress. Her luscious sable hair was disheveled, and lying haphazardly around her shoulders. Gone was the ponytail. It looked as if fingers had been run through the heavy locks. Had Sinclair done that while he made love to her? Jake scowled and silently cursed at the thought.

There were dark hollows beneath her eyes as if she hadn't slept in days. Her forehead creased into a frown. She nervously licked her lips—which were devoid of lipstick—and clasped her hands together. His wife, he thought with disdain, coming straight from another man's bed. But he still wanted her—needed her—loved her.

The last time they'd made love hinged at the edges of his mind. He remembered taking her in the heat and insanity of lost control, devouring her in their bed amongst the tumultuous madness of tangled sheets, sweat, and raw sex. It'd been weeks since he touched her but it felt like years.

He grunted in disgust and pushed the thoughts aside.

"It's after midnight." He burrowed deeper into his chair, afraid if he stood, he wouldn't last long on his feet. The scattered emotions running through him would be his undoing.

He spared a hard look at his wife. He was cynic and knew it. Women had always come to him easily and he took advantage of that fact. But Melissa had been different.

"I know," she said.

He stared at her.

He hadn't believed in the sanctity of monogamous relationships. Past encounters had colored his outlook on faithfulness. But when he met Melissa, he'd gladly given up serial one-night stands and cold relationships with women friends who knew not to expect anything from him. He made sure he left them completely satisfied sexually.

Regret stabbed at him and he didn't like the feeling. He wasn't a man to look backward. He didn't try to sugar coat what he had been, a cold-hearted son of a bitch, but the past was the past and there wasn't a damn thing he could do to change it. But he had changed— Melissa had done that.

Jake stood, drained the liquor, and moved to fill his glass again. He sipped at the liquid, waiting for the numbness to set in. It didn't. The emptiness of the last few weeks nagged at him. He'd purposely distanced himself from Melissa. Partly because he was angry, but more importantly, he didn't want to be around when he lost her.

"You seem surprised to see me." Jake placed the glass on the high end table, strolled toward her with his hands in his pockets.

"I am," she said, softly.

Her chin was raised and her eyes were staring into his. He almost smiled at the defiant stance but not quite. Melissa always had a backbone and could be stubborn.

"I don't see why. I do live here," he said.

"Really? I hadn't noticed since you made sure you were gone before I came down in the mornings."

"Ah, you either missed me or you're pissed. Which is it?"

She inhaled deeply. "That all you have to say—this isn't a joke."

"I don't hear myself laughing, lady. Where the hell were you tonight?"

Surprise crossed her face, but disappeared as quickly as it came. Was it guilt? He watched as she composed herself. Now her face was blank of all expression, shutting him out. He felt isolated.

"I worked late."

"And—"

"I went to dinner."

"With whom?"

She paused. His heart flipped hard in his chest, causing the breath in his lungs to catch in an excruciating grip. Would she lie?

"With a friend."

"Where?"

Her gaze narrowed. "Why the third degree?"

He continued. "Man or woman?"

No more retreating behind a shield. The rules had changed. He was fighting to win, but he wouldn't abide a lie.

She took a long breath and exhaled. "I had dinner with Brent."

"Where?"

"His hotel." Her voice was barely audible.

"In the restaurant?"

He waited.

His mind screamed, please don't lie.

"No."

His heart pounded and he exhaled the trapped air lounged in his lungs. He crossed his arms, trying to appear relaxed and waited for her to continue.

"In his suite." she said calmly, as if she'd been having dinner with a casual friend instead of her ex-lover who had also been her husband.

"I know." He kept his voice cool and deliberate.

"You know?" She frowned. "What were you doing, having me followed?"

"Didn't have to. I was there having a business meeting with a client."

Her eyes widened. "Why didn't you say something?"

"How could I? You hurried to the elevator and got in with Sinclair before I could make my presence known."

"I see."

He walked to her, almost touching her. She stood still, not moving, as he got up in her face. Was she afraid of him now? He steeled himself against the fear and misery that was trying to wrap itself around him. He let anger have free rein.

"Do you? The two of you were engrossed in each other. If the damn hotel caught fire you wouldn't have known it. I could've broken his *motherfucking* neck. You're lucky, lady, the elevator door shut when it did," he spit out.

"What's gotten into you?" She backed up and then moved away from him. "We had dinner—that's all."

He grabbed her arm, pulling her back toward him. "You were in a hotel room with your lover for hours and I'm supposed to believe all you did was have dinner."

"He's not my lover."

He ignored her denial. "Then you come home disheveled,

looking like you just rolled out of his bed."

She wrenched her arm from his grasp. "That's disgusting." Her expression was a blend of hurt and shock. "I haven't done anything to warrant your abuse. I won't stand for you telling me I did. Whose bed have you been sleeping in? Because it damn sure hasn't been mine."

"You expect me to sleep with the two of you?"

"You're crazy."

"By the looks of you, I know something happened. Did you fuck him?"

Emotion, silence and tension vibrated through the room. Only the loud ringing of his iPhone cut through it.

"It's after midnight." She glared at him. "Must be one of your whores."

She moved to the opened door.

"Don't walk out on me. We haven't finished."

Without another word, she left the room.

"Damn," he murmured, looked at the phone, and hit Connect for the overseas call.

CHAPTER SEVEN

Damn him! Melissa slammed the master bedroom door. Pissed, she mumbled as she removed her clothes, dropped them on the floor and walked toward the bathroom. Her body shook with unbridled anger. Who the hell did he think he was talking to her like that? He was the only one who could ignite her temper to raging proportions quicker than a runaway house fire.

She wanted a bath to soothe away the tension but since it was late she would settle for a hot shower.

She ground her teeth. He was bull-headed and arrogant, but to accuse her of sleeping with Brent made her madder than hell.

Granted, she hadn't known what to expect when Brent told her they would be having dinner in his suite, but she knew no matter the circumstance or situation, she wouldn't have forgotten her marriage vows. Although she'd allowed Brent to kiss her, she hadn't been tempted to sleep with him. Jake should've known that.

Why would he, she asked herself. Since seeing Brent in Jake's office, she'd been off-kilter—confused and unsure of what she was feeling. Damn. She expected him to understand, to give her room to sort it all out, not to brand her an adulteress.

Stepping out of the shower, she wrapped a towel around her body and returned to the bedroom. The door opened. Jake entered, newly showered and wearing the bottoms of a pair of pajamas only. Hell, if he didn't look good. It had been weeks, hell, close to a month since they made love. She looked past him at the wall to keep him from seeing how his presence affected her equilibrium. He appeared relaxed and self-confident, but she knew better. He may be confident, but he was far from relaxed. He moved like a lion, silently stalking his prey.

Melissa tried to ignore him and moving to her dressing table, grabbed the lotion, and sat to apply the lavender cream to her arms and legs, making sure to keep the towel in place. Her nerves were stretched to the limit but would be damned if she would let him know it. He stood in the middle of the bedroom, watching with his arms crossed.

"What do you want, Jake?"

"We'll now continue our conversation," he said.

"I'm tired." She placed the lotion bottle on the makeup table, stood and reached for the robe on the back of the chair. She turned away and silently started counting. She slipped her arms through the satin sleeves, dropped the towel and belted the robe. When she reached the number fifty, she turned and faced him.

"Not tonight. Please leave. I'm getting ready to go to bed."

"So, am I." Coolly, he unfolded his arms and moved to his side of the bed.

"You're not sleeping here, Jake."

"Watch me." He threw the decorative pillows to the floor, and pulled back the comforter and sheet. "We'll no longer sleep in separate rooms. From now on, we share a bed."

She raised her chin. "You want to sleep with a woman who just came from another man's bed?"

"What the hell are you saying?" His tone was hard.

"You asked if I fucked Brent."

"Did you?"

"*Fuck* you, Jake!"

The silence was a heavy dense fog.

Melissa sighed wearily. "If you want the bed, you can have it." She hurried toward the door, but he stepped in front her.

His cold, gray eyes bore down on her. "You rushed to take a shower. Why? To wash the scent of Sinclair from your body?"

"I'm tired of this." She stepped back. "You're insane. How many times do I have to say it? I. Didn't. Sleep. With. Brent."

"You expect me to believe that?" He laughed cruelly. "His cologne is all over you."

"We greeted each other. I'm sure you saw that in the lobby."

"Yes, I saw it. It looked like the two of you could barely wait for the bedroom."

She trembled with anger. "You're disgusting. You are reaching. Maybe it's to cover your dirt. "

"What the hell are you talking about?"

"You came home covered in a woman's perfume."

"So is this payback."

"That's your MO not mine."

"Something else happened and I want to know what it was."

"I won't stand for you cross-examining me. *I'm going to tell you this once* and I won't speak of it again. Brent and I had dinner. We talked. We hugged each other good-bye."

"Did you kiss him?"

"We were married and friends for a long time."

"That's no damn answer."

"That's the only answer you're getting."

Anger still boiling inside her veins, she refused to give him a definitive answer. Let him stew about it.

"You're my wife, Melissa. Not his. I don't share."

"But I'm supposed to share you with other women, is that it?"

"It was never an issue until you changed the rules."

"So you admit to sleeping with another woman."

"Now who's doing the cross-examining?"

"I won't overlook infidelity, Jake."

"I won't either."

They stared at each other for a long time. Neither willing to back down.

She took a deep breath and then planted her hands on her hips. "I kissed Brent. It happened. I can't change it. Maybe it was reflex, the past, memories, I don't know. I'm sorry, but I'm not going to pay the rest of my life for it. I need space. Please move out of my way."

His eyes flashed with an emotion she couldn't identify and as quickly as it appeared it was gone. He might be able to pretend what they shared these last few months was nothing more than good sex—damn, it was great sex. She'd made a mistake with Brent. All she had to do was make her husband believe it.

Before she could ask him again to move, he scooped her into his arms and walked quickly to the bed.

"Jake," she yelped. "What are you doing?"

"What does it look like I'm doing?"

"This isn't going to happen," she said as he dropped her unceremoniously on the bed. "I'm not having sex with you. We have too many unsolved issues. Sex won't make them go away."

"We're not having sex," he stated.

"Good." She scrambled to leave the bed but he stopped her.

A voice strained and rough with need that was barely audible said. "I want to make love to you. I've been without you too long, baby. I ache." He stared down at her for along moment. "I haven't dishonored my marriage vows."

She swallowed with relief.

"I'm asking for one night. One with no barriers, accusations, or who's right or wrong. Will you give me that?" he said.

"It won't change anything. There's no trust between us. At one time I thought we had that, but we don't." She ran a weary hand through her tangled locks. "You accused me of cheating on you. If you don't know what kind of person I am, what do we have?"

He threw a furtive glance as he stood staring down at her with his hands at his waist. It made her uncomfortable so she swung her feet to the side of the bed and stood. Moving toward the dressing table, she kept occupied arranging the bottles of lotion and creams into neat lines.

"Will you please look at me, Melissa?"

She turned and faced him.

He pierced her with his gaze. "We are married. It's a partnership. I thought we also had trust. Then an ex-husband, who I knew nothing about, shows up."

"I'm sorry. I should've told you about Brent."

"I agree."

Exasperated, she threw up her hands. "I'm finished with this conversation."

"Bullshit. I'm not. I want to know why it's taken you weeks to remember you're married."

"Damn, Jake. You're like a dog with a bone. No matter how many times I tell you to let it go, you won't. I've tried to explain but you won't listen. How many times do I have to apologize?"

"I don't remember you apologizing previously."

"Alright! I apologize. I'm sorry! For keeping my previous marriage a secret, for kissing Brent, for having dinner with him.

Satisfied? But it's my past not yours. It had nothing to do with you."

He moved toward her. "Nothing to do with me? The hell it didn't. I made some missteps here. One, I gave you the space you needed. That was my first mistake. Secondly, I sat back and waited for you to make a decision. Third, I let you be in charge of the situation. No more. You belong to me and it's time you realize it. I'm putting my foot down—"

She laughed. "Your what?"

"You think it's funny?'

She regarded him silently for a long moment. Never had she seen Jake act this way. He was normally so cool, confident and unmovable, when it came to emotions.

She approached him and placed her hand to his cheek. He stiffened. A smile almost crossed her lips when his eyes widened at her gesture. But he quickly averted his gaze, not letting her see anything beyond his mask. She'd never made the first move in the entire time they had been together. Never. Not a kiss, not a touch, nor had she initiated their lovemaking. The fear of rejection had stopped her. She surprised herself as she stroked his jawline. With boldness she ran her fingers across his firm lips. His breathing ragged, she felt it caress her hand, warm and moist.

Strong fingers fastened firmly on her wrist, stopping her progress. His eyes temporarily lost their fierceness. His expression was softer—but nonetheless dangerous. Melissa realized a battle was warring inside of him.

"You ask for so much sometimes, loyalty, trust and straight answers. Everything isn't always black or white, Jake. But then there are times you ask for so little. I wonder if I'll ever really know you."

"There's where you are wrong, baby. You know me *very* well."

With that said, he placed his mouth over hers. Momentarily, she was paralyzed by the raw power of the kiss.

He lifted his head, his glittering gray eyes roaming her face. An intangible thread of something—was it sadness or pain? She couldn't tell. Then everything changed. Had she imagined what she had seen? Then the hard lines of his face spoke of a man who was in in charge once again.

He kissed her hard, this time with possessiveness. She fought to breathe. A flush of heat suffused her body. Despite the misgivings that plagued her about their marriage, she leaned into him, seeking his warmth. He groaned and deepened the kiss. She felt herself being lifted, her robe falling around her shoulders, and then she was straddling his thighs. He laid her gently on the bed, his mouth still fused with hers. Their tongues met and tangled in a battle for ownership. He moved slowly as if he had all the time in the world to accomplish his mission. He was the only man she knew who treated kissing like it was the most important element of loving.

He broke the kiss for a moment, his lips sliding apart in a slow movement. His lips glided lightly over her cheek, her eyes, her nose and then her temple. Her breath caught at the softness—tenderness of the gesture. The moment was suspended in memory. It said he'd missed her. She also missed him—the connection—the fierce passion. Coolness hit her skin when he removed her robe, leaving her bare to his touch and eyes.

"Jake," she whispered, the quietness around them feeling almost peaceful.

"It's been too damn long."

"Aww, Jake," she squirmed when he captured her nipple.

"Shh." He gave her gentle, lingering kisses all over her breasts, neck and face between words. "I want us both to enjoy this. We won't if you continue to touch me. I want you too bad. I'm afraid I have no control, sweetheart."

Jake Sorenson was a tough man. He didn't show emotions or speak of what he wanted; he just took it. For him to admit he needed her was telling in itself.

Sheila had warned her when her and Jake's relationship was new that he didn't do cozy and sensitive episodes with women. He was very candid and to the point about what he wanted without having to say much. He could be critical without remorse. Whatever anger he was feeling hadn't abated his desire at all.

She grabbed his head, bringing his lips to hers once again. He let her be the initiator for several minutes but she knew it wouldn't last. Allowing her tongue to tease his, she felt the gesture surprised and excited him. She tunneled her fingers through his gorgeous hair, pulling him to the heat. The pressure of his hard penis pushed at the wet opening of her vagina. When had he discarded his pajamas bottoms? She inhaled deeply, clawing at his back, trying to make him complete the act. He held her hips in place.

Melissa felt the powerful rawness touching her clit. All she knew was that she wanted him—now. With Jake, sex was wild and free. Their need for each other was predatory in nature, hot and explosive. He lifted, moved her further up on the bed and opened her legs, wide.

His hands were everywhere initiating emotions she didn't think were possible. Lost in a haze of pleasure, she almost blurted out that she loved him, but she couldn't. He wouldn't believe her—at least not now but soon. First, they had to clear the obstacles in their path.

Masculine fingers caressed her opening, circling her clit folds before moving to mold her breasts and pluck her nipples.

Raw sounds of need slipped from her mouth to his. Her body shuddered at the sensation, sharp talons of sexual thirst gripping tightly and making her muscles strain with release.

Again he caressed her swollen clitoris, inserting one finger—then two—and finally three. The pleasure built at lightning speed and Melissa felt her climax explode into fragments of raw heat, clawing her insides. She moaned, knowing she was near the edge. His kiss swallowed her scream before it could escape.

He moved away. The night stand drawer opened and a condom wrapper tore. Lazily, she opened her eyes just enough to see the animalistic carnality of his face. She grew more wet and swollen. Her insides clenched in undeniable hunger. He thrust inside her in one mind-blowing stroke, filling her like no other man could. She could barely catch her breath. He took her as if he was laying claim. It was primitive. Melissa was his—Jake was hers. At this moment no shadows stood between them.

Breathing hard, he looked down at her, his eyes dark with desire. "You okay?"

She answered with a tilt of her pelvis, taking him deeper into her womb.

He pumped at a slow pace, teasing her, and then with hard powerful strokes, claiming her. With each plunge he took her higher and higher.

"Look at me Melissa," he muttered. "Tell me you want me."

His demand, his strong thrusts and all the love she was experiencing were too much. Her body clenched him.

"Tell me," he groaned.

She rotated her hips. "I want you...I want you."

"Say my name."

"Ah, Jake...Jake."

He plunged deeper and swelled.

She gasped at the fullness.

A deep spasm of pleasure released her into an atmosphere of ecstasy.

He continued with deep strokes through her orgasm, hitting her G-spot with inflexible pressure. Finally, he stiffened and swore, shuddering into a powerful climax with her name on his lips.

"Melissa..."

Feeling his heartbeat pound against hers, she didn't want to let him go. Something had changed at that moment.

She met his gaze as he rolled to lie beside her. He threw an arm across his eyes, breathing deep and fast. She turned toward him and continued to watch him in silence. He leaned over and rubbed his mouth against hers then arranged her in his arms. The loving gesture took her by surprise.

"Jake,—" she started, but didn't know what to say.

"Go to sleep, Melissa."

"But—"

He kissed her again, silencing anything that would've come out of her mouth.

"Rest."

He tucked her firmly across his chest, pulled a sheet over them, and relaxed his eyes. She lay listening to him breathe and felt the strong beat of his heart pulsating against her cheek.

Physically, their lovemaking had been unbelievable, but there'd been something deeper tonight. Did she imagine it? Could she dare hope things would be different now? Finally, she drifted into a dreamless sleep.

CHAPTER EIGHT

Slowly Melissa opened her eyes to the bright light coming through the open drapes. She squinted, grabbed the pillows to cover her head, and groaned. Then it hit her...Jake. She shot straight up in bed, the sheet falling from around her naked body.

Jake's side of the bed was empty. She placed her hand where he'd lain. It was cool to the touch. Evidently, he'd been gone a long time. The hands on the clock read well past seven a.m., which meant he'd already left the house. She sighed and fell back among the tousled bed coverings.

Lying there for a moment, her mind ran over the events of last night. Jake had been angry and it didn't help matters when her temper spiked to match his. They were supposed to talk but ended up making love all through the night. She tossed back the covers, and headed to the bathroom. Having sex, no matter how great, didn't solve their problems. It was about time he knew that. There was no trust, at least on his part, when it came to her. But as usual, he was too pig-headed to listen to reason. No more. She would make him listen even if she had to lock him in his office.

Stepping out of the shower, she heard the phone ring in the bedroom. She hurried to answer it, hoping it was Jake.

"Hello," she said breathlessly, holding the towel in place.

"Melissa?"

Disappointed, she sighed. "Hi, Brent."

"You don't sound like yourself."

"I'm fine. Why are you calling? I thought we said everything we needed to say last night."

"I'm on my way to the airport now." He paused for a moment. "I wanted to say good-bye." He paused for another moment. "Again, I want to say how sorry I am about everything."

"Brent, you're not a person who repeats himself. What is the real reason for this call?"

"Just wanted to make sure you're okay?"

Impatiently, she retorted, "You can do better than that."

She waited for him to get to the point. Silence came through the line.

"Sorensen has a reputation in business for not being forgiving. He's a hard man. I'm positive he's not a man who takes kindly to his wife coming home past midnight."

"He would never hurt me, Brent. Yeah, he can be conservative and unbending in some aspects, but he doesn't let his anger rule him."

"So, he was angry?" he said slowly as if he knew what had happened between her and Jake.

"My husband is off limits." She took a deep breath. "Look, I have to go."

She was glad they had come to an amicable place. They didn't belong in each other's future.

"Brent, thanks for calling. Have a safe flight."

She severed the connection without giving him another thought.

⁓

"Where in the hell is he?" she murmured, as his private phone line continued to ring in his office.

She had walked to Jake's office three times within the last hour and also called him. He still wasn't there. Where could he be, she pondered again as she hung up the phone.

She didn't want to ask his assistant. For one thing, the man would've given her an inquisitive stare. He and Jake's personalities matched—cranky, curt, and brooding. That's probably why they got along so well.

Her assistant, Joan walked through the door. "Melissa, since Jake is in New York, could you sign these documents? I need to Express them overnight to the client." She handed the papers to Melissa.

Shock caused her to stiffen. "Jake's in New York?"

Joan frowned. "Yes. You didn't know?"

Melissa rubbed at the tension in her temples. "Ah, I must've forgotten," she lied. "I have so much on my mind and too many deadlines."

"You two live in the same house, don't you?" Joan joked.

"We are so busy, we barely see each other.'

At least that was the truth.

"Is there anything I can do to lighten the load? I could stay a couple hours after work this week."

Melissa signed the contracts and handed them to her. "No. You don't have to. I'm fine."

"Okay." Her assistant turned to leave.

"Joan." Melissa stopped her. "Ah...uh...Could you tell me which hotel Jake is staying?"

Her friend and employee looked at her.

A riot of emotions were churning inside Melissa, one of them being embarrassment.

"He's staying at the Waldorf." She paused for a moment. "I could get more information from his assistant." She waited.

Melissa slowly nodded. "Thank you. I would appreciate that."

⌒

"I should call Jake and let him know I'm coming," Melissa said to Sheila, as she folded lingerie in the suitcase. It had been a week since she last saw Jake. She admitted to herself that she missed him a great deal.

"No, you're not. Surprise is the best medicine for my cousin. It would do him good. His life is too orderly. The axle he sits on needs to be tilted a little." She laughed.

Sheila grabbed a handful of grapes from the bowl she'd brought into the bedroom. She munched loudly. Melissa grinned. Her pregnant friend thought it was her right to eat anything she wanted. It was good she had a high metabolism.

"Has Jake called?"

"He left a message," Melissa said. She didn't want to say it was a note left on the nightstand by their bed. The note had said he would be in meetings and unavailable, but nothing about the meetings being in New York. It bothered her he didn't at least phone when he'd arrived at his hotel. Something was wrong. She just didn't know what was going on in Jake's head right now.

"A message? Is that all?" Sheila inquired.

She ignored the questions.

"Jake wants to open an office in New York."

Sheila frowned. "I thought it was only in the planning stage."

"He moved up the negotiations."

"I didn't know that. But that shouldn't have stopped him from calling."

She agreed but didn't voice it.

Melissa offered, cautiously. "Maybe there was a snag in the negotiations. I don't want to go and get in the way."

"You won't get in the way. He could probably use your negotiating skills."

"I don't know. Maybe—"

"What's wrong? You act as if you don't want to go."

"That's not it."

"Then what is?"

She snapped the suitcase shut and put it by the bedroom door.

"This thing with Brent caused a serious bump in our relationship." She paused a moment. "Jake left for New York without telling me."

"What?"

She refused to tell Sheila that they'd made love and she foolishly thought everything was fine between them.

"Jake's a proud man with a huge ego. He's always been that way. But, he'll come around. He loves you."

Melissa's mouth dropped open. "What did you say?"

Sheila laughed. "Come on. You know Jake loves you." She squinted. "Don't you?"

"We care about each other. We even respect each other. But love..."

"Are you serious?" Her friend's expression was almost comical. "I don't care what reasons he gave you for proposing. It was love. Pure and simple."

"Your pregnancy is making you delusional."

Sheila was Jake's cousin, but Melissa was his wife. She knew her husband, or thought she did until he left her. He was complicated, deeply complex, a hunter. Driven. Nothing stood in his way. He'd married her for his own reasons and she did the same. He felt it was time to settle down with a woman who complemented him in bed. One that could hold an intelligent conversation whether it be personal or business. But who also had people and social skills. She had those qualities. Jake didn't. He was impatient and didn't see the need for idle chit-chat or conversation. He wanted children, which surprised her, but made her happy. She wanted a large family—one day.

Jake was tough. There was nothing soft and fuzzy about him. She understood and accepted love wasn't in his DNA.

"You call me delusional?" Sheila covered her pregnant belly. "Watch your tongue. You shouldn't talk like that in front of your godchild. You're going to give her a complex."

"A girl?"

"Don't change the subject."

"You're solely mistaken about Jake." Melissa hoped this would end any nonsense about Jake loving her.

"For years I've observed Jake watching you when he didn't think anyone was looking. He wanted you from the beginning. Way before the two of you started dating. He was like a lion waiting for the right time to approach his prey. I confronted him about his feelings."

Wide-eyed, Melissa asked. "You did what?"

Sheila shrugged. "He never denied them. He just listened in that cold, brooding way of his. Shrewd eyes, a tight jaw and pinched lips." Sheila laughed. "Jake hates it when I read him."

"I can understand why. He's a very private person. But, I still believe you are way off base. Jake Sorenson isn't in love with me. He's never given any indication our relationship was more than what we decided it would be."

"Both of you are too stubborn. Stop beating around the bush and tell Jake you love him."

"I—"

"You do love him, don't you, Melissa?"

She paused. She did love him but it was a complicated love filled with problems. But she admitted to herself it didn't change her feelings about him.

Silence in the room hung between them.

"It's not as simple as black or white."

"I didn't say it was. Do you love him?" she asked again. This time with urgency.

"Yes, but—"

Sheila clapped her hands like a giddy child. "I knew it! I'm glad you stopped hiding behind what your ex-husband did to you."

"Brent and I had a long talk. We're in a good place. It still doesn't mean Jake and I will end up being this happily ever after couple. I don't believe in fairytales any longer. "

"The love between you and Jake is real."

"Sheila..."

"And lots of *real hot* sex. Sex is the glue that can solve a mountain of problems. Well, at least some of the times."

"Only you would think that. You are a sex addict. You need therapy." She shook her head.

"True to the sex addiction and no to therapy."

"You're a bona fide crazy woman."

"Thank you." Sheila hugged her. Then she picked up the scarf she'd thrown across the chair near the bed and wrapped it around her shoulders. "Are you ready? You don't want to miss your flight."

Melissa absently grabbed a light-weight jacket. Jake in love with her? She laughed softly to herself. Impossible.

"You'll need something heavier for New York. It's October, you know."

"I'll be fine."

"Don't say I didn't warn you."

Melissa laughed. "Come on let's go.

CHAPTER NINE

All Jake wanted to do was to rip off his tie, grab a scotch, and sleep. He'd been in New York for over a week negotiating a contract to open a new office. He was tired. The negotiations had been long and tedious. He'd prolonged them longer than necessary. He hadn't wanted to return to Los Angeles to meet his wife's accusing eyes. Their long night of lovemaking couldn't erase all the doubts in his mind. But the memory of how she surrendered to fierce need to mate caused his penis to swell. Damn. He needed to get a grip.

Anger still swirled his insides. Her connection to Sinclair ate at his gut.

Now he sat at the dinner table, in the hotel restaurant with his financial director and friend, Matthew Connor. Also in attendance was the former owner of the office complex he'd just bought and one of the man's high-priced lawyers. A tall, statuesque blonde-haired woman with large green eyes, a sharp negotiator with brains and beauty, she oozed confidence. He'd first met her a year ago when he came to New York for the initial meeting with the owner of the complex. She made a play for him then and he'd ignored it. He was with Melissa and didn't want or need another woman. How his life had changed in a year. It now mocked him.

She was an extremely beautiful woman. She knew it and used it to her advantage.

She was powerful.

She was seduction.

She was tough.

She went after whatever she wanted—at this moment— it was him.

It was evident in her speech. Her direct approach was strong, but subtle. Bridget Manley didn't deal in bullshit, could hang with the elite and get down in the gutter with the rats. She played to win but so did he.

All week he'd felt the sexual vibes she threw his way. He hadn't responded to their heated bantering, but had silently enjoyed it. It was his last night in New York. Without acknowledging it, he knew she expected to end up in his bed. He observed her as he drank expensive 1996 Dom Perignon, thinking how the night may play out. No matter what—he would decide the outcome.

He grimaced as the bubbly and expensive champagne slid down his throat. No matter how many times he drank the stuff, he'd never acquired a taste for it. He would rather have a glass of Macallan scotch. It was his drink of choice. But tonight he was supposed to be in a celebratory mood.

Well, he wasn't. He was irritable and wanted to get the hell up from the table and go home. Damn. Then he remembered he couldn't go home—not yet. Leaving Melissa asleep in their bed wouldn't sit well. He had a lot of explaining to do. Many times he found himself reaching for the phone during the week, but he stopped himself. He wanted her to miss him. Not only that, he didn't want to hear her decision about her ex-husband. Shit. He ran like a little boy afraid of his shadow. There were too many unanswered questions. Like, could she love him? Could they have a *real* marriage? Would she choose him over Sinclair? Damn. He was pathetic. He'd never begged a woman before. He wouldn't start now. Hell. Who was he kidding? He would do anything to win her.

"What do you say, Jake?" Bridget leaned into him, her breast caressing his arm. A soft hand laid over his, while the other caressed his inner thigh near his crotch.

"About what?" He stiffened, reached under the table and removed her hand. Bridget knew he was married. Although he hadn't said it, the bold gold band on his finger said it all.

The tightening at the corner of her mouth spoke volumes.

What was he doing? He was married. Mad as hell at his wife. But, damn, a night of mindless sex wouldn't erase Melissa from his thoughts or his heart. How far was he willing to go to forget his troubles for just a little while?

"To go dancing. There's a wonderful night club in this hotel." She rubbed against him again and actually purred.

"Not tonight." He looked at his friend who wore a sly grin on his face. "I'm sure Matthew would love to go."

He held up his hand. "Oh, no. I don't dance. It's not something I've ever accomplished."

Matthew and he had been friends since their freshman year in college. Besides his cousin Sheila, no one knew him as well. There was a smirk on his face that indicated he knew the woman beside him was in serious heat.

He was as tall as Jake with premature salt-and-peppered hair. He was fit. Exercise was his drug of choice.

His fiancée had died suddenly from a brain aneurysm when he

was twenty-eight years old. That had been almost twelve years ago. Jake hadn't seen him in a relationship since then. He was never without woman companionship, however never with the same woman twice. But it didn't keep women from trying to stake a claim. He was rich, handsome and gallant. Melissa had told him once that besides Matthew's good looks, it was the gallant part that drew the women like bees.

Jake frowned. "You're only one year older than me."

Matthew chuckled. "That said." He drained the champagne in his glass. "I'm heading up to my room." He stood. "I'm flying out tomorrow morning so I'll say my good-byes now." He saluted everyone at the table. "I'll see you back in L.A., Jake."

The older gentleman got to his feet also. "Wait up, Mr. Connor. I'll walk out with you. I told my wife I'd be home an hour ago."

Jake stood and the man shook his hand. "Mr. Sorenson, I'll send the final papers to you overnight when they are completed."

"Thank you."

He hesitated, glanced at Bridget, and then back to Jake. "Okay. Good-night then."

Jake signaled for the waiter and sat back down. "Bring me a bottle of your top shelf scotch."

The server tilted his head in acknowledgement and walked away.

Bridget flung her hair over her shoulder. "Scotch? That's a little strong for this late in the evening, don't you think?" She eyed him curiously.

"If you want more champagne, I'll order another bottle."

"No, scotch is fine."

The silence hung between them.

The waiter returned with the bottle, opened it, and started to pour. Jake stopped him. "Thank you. I'll take it from here."

Jake stood with the bottle in his hand. Bridget came to her feet also and smoothed her tight red dress around her slim hips. She waited. Without exchanging words, they moved toward the elevators.

At the door of his suite, Jake stepped back and allowed her to enter. Closing the door, he moved to the mini-bar, took a glass and filled it to the brim with scotch. He gulped it down in one swift movement.

"Whoa, lover." She laughed. "I don't want you drunk. At least not until I've sampled the goods." Bridget ran her hands seductively down his back. He turned around, shrugged out of his suit jacket, loosened his tie and threw both of them on a chair. She pulled the shirt from his pants and proceeded to unbutton it. In her haste, buttons fell to the floor.

"Damn. I can't wait." Her breathing was erratic and deep.

She shimmed. The dress dropped around her feet. She kicked it from around her ankles. Jake stepped back, narrowed his gaze and observed her for a long moment.

Before him stood a well-endowed woman with curves in the right places, sexy and probably damn good in the sheets. She was braless. He surmised she had some work done to enhance her breasts. They were ripe. Her areolas hard and pointed. A slight pulse shot through his dick. But none of the full-blown hardness he expected.

She ran her hands down his chest and flicked his nipples. He stood completely still. She was in heat, at a fevered pitch. It only irritated him. When she reached for the buckle on his slacks, he grabbed her hands and pushed them away.

"No."

She blinked. "What?"

"You need to leave." He retrieved her dress from the floor, handing it to her.

"Leave? Are you kidding me?" she shouted, tossing the dress on the chair alongside his tie and jacket.

His gaze scanned her feminine curves. She had a slender waist, inviting hips and long, lithe legs that would wrap around any man's waist while he found his pleasure. There was only one problem—he wasn't interested. All he could see was a petite woman, with large brown eyes, dark sable locks that caressed her neck and creamy mocha chocolate skin.

Driven by anger and ego, he'd made a huge mistake tonight. He tried to replace what he really wanted, his wife, with another woman. He loved Melissa and damn if he wasn't going to fight for her. He picked up Bridget's dress again and put it into her hands.

"I'll have my driver take you wherever you want. This here." He pointed at her and then himself. "It's not happening."

She snatched the dress. "What fucking game are you playing? All week you've been coming on to me. Now you have cold feet?" she shouted.

Jake rested his hands at his hips and glared. He considered himself the master of his emotions. He only allowed people to see what he wanted them to see, but right now he didn't give a damn. He wanted her gone.

"The conversation isn't up for debate. This was a mistake. "

"You think this is how it's going to end?" She threw at him. "No man has ever said no to me. I'll be damned if you'll be the first."

He moved into her space. "I admit I liked the attention. I'm sorry I let it get this far. Don't make this harder than it already is. Put your dress on. You need to leave...now."

She glanced passed his shoulder and laughed. "Oh, I see you want a threesome?" Bridget wrapped her arms around his neck and kissed him hard, biting his lip in the process.

"What the hell do—" He pulled her hands from around him and pushed her away. "Get the fuck out!" He wiped his mouth with the back of his hand. His temper was beyond his reach.

If she didn't leave now he would throw her ass out.

She continued to laugh, nodded and pointed at something past his shoulder. He turned to see what the hell she was looking at.

"Who's the bitch in heat, Jake?" A dry tone filtered from across the room.

In the doorway of the bedroom, his beautiful wife stood with her hands propped on her hips, looking disgusted and mad as hell—and wounded.

CHAPTER TEN

Despair cruised through Melissa's body at a slow speed and then built to a crescendo of pain. She stood rooted to the spot in the archway of the bedroom door, hoping the devastation she was feeling wasn't evident on her face.

Only a small flicker of shock crossed Jake's face. If she hadn't been looking at him she would've missed it. Her husband now stood stoic, without any sign of emotion. His shirt laid open, his bare chest hard and rippled with abs any younger man would fight for. She turned away from the sight. Then she spared him another glance noticing the swelling to his bottom lip. The sight almost made her sick to her stomach. He'd kissed the blonde-haired whore. Not a soft kiss but a hungry one.

His eyes were trained on her.

No emotion.

No embarrassment.

No guilt.

Nothing.

She was afraid if she moved from where she stood, she would fall flat on her face, so she leaned against the door with her arms crossed, hoping it would help to renew her strength.

"Who the hell are you calling a bitch?" the woman squealed and hurried toward her. Jake reached out and stopped her progression.

"Don't even think about it." he growled.

Melissa walked toward them. She would be damned if she would let either of them see her cower. She moved, remembering to put one foot in front of the other and stopped a few feet before she reached them, making sure she kept space between them and her. She feared she would crumble, so she didn't look at Jake again.

Melissa eyed the green-eyed woman before her. She hated to admit it, but she was gorgeous, tall and busty. This was the type of woman Jake dated in the past.

"I didn't know you like brown sugar, Jake." The bitch snatched her arm from him, stepped into her dress and pulled the straps haphazardly over her shoulders. She threw Jake a short nod. "He might want a threesome." She flung her long hair over her shoulder. "But, not tonight sweetie. He's all mine."

"Really? What does he say about it?" Melissa said.

She still didn't look at Jake. She was afraid if she did she would slap the shit out of him. How could he do this to her?

"Bridget..."

So the bitch had a name—and he knew it. The wound deepened. This was no one-night stand.

Jake grabbed Bridget's arm, ushering her toward the door. "Leave."

"What about her? If I'm leaving so is she."

"No, she's not."

She pushed at his hand, but he kept a firm grip on her arm. "I'm not leaving," she said, glaring at Melissa. "Who the hell are you anyway?"

Melissa lifted her brow, but didn't answer.

"She's my wife." He threw open the door. "Now leave."

"Well, well, I didn't believe you were married. I thought the ring you wore was a deterrent to keep women at bay. You're certainly a surprise, Jake."

"Now you know." He shut the door in her face.

He leaned against the door, watching her with hooded eyes. Melissa walked up to him and slapped him as hard as she could across his face. The bastard didn't flinch. He just stood there. Arrogant. Bold. Unashamed. It made her blood boil.

"Did that make you feel better?" he asked, calmly.

"You son of a bitch." She balled up her fist and punched him in his gut. Then she started screaming, cursing, crying, and all the while she continued to hit him. He stood there and took the blows. Winded and her heart filled with agony, she slid towards the floor. Tears washed her face. Her vision blurred. He caught her in his arms before she landed on the carpet and held her against his chest. For a long time, she just cried hard, lost in the misery that consumed her.

She wanted to be loved. Her parents, Brent and now Jake, they had all rejected her. No more would she seek love. She didn't need it. She could live without it.

She twisted her body, trying to move out of his arms. "Let me go, Jake."

"No." His arms clamped tight in a protective hold.

"Let. Me. Go."

He didn't.

She pushed hard against his chest. "You're going to hold me against my will?"

He released her, a grim look on his face. He ran his hand

wearily over the back of his head. "I would never hurt you, sweetheart."

She rounded on him, fresh angry tears sprang in her eyes. She screamed. "Don't. You. Ever. Call. Me. That. Again." She pointed a finger at him. "I'm not your damn sweetheart, honey, darling, whatever other terms you want to use. Save it for the whores that frequent your bed."

"Since the first moment I saw you, I never took another woman to my bed. You know that."

"I caught you red-handed, Jake. The woman was naked."

"I know what it looks like but nothing happened. You need to listen."

"I don't need to do a damn thing." She ran a hand across her eyes, fighting the tears. No more tears. Not in front of him. Was this to be her life? Burning heat radiated through her veins, her stomach churned and her heart felt as if it would explode.

"What was tonight?"

"A mistake."

"You're a liar. The great Jake Sorensen doesn't make mistakes like normal people. Every move you ever make is calculated. I know you. Tonight was calculated."

His jaws tightened; a red tinge fanned his face. The tension flared thick between them. But he remained silent, which only fueled her anger more.

She turned away, her arms stiff at her sides and wiped her face again with the back of her hand. The air left her lungs, like she'd been punched in the stomach. Melissa struggled to breathe but her body fought to deny her to do so. Choppy, rapid breaths escaped her while she struggled not to drown. She felt Jake behind her, not touching, but near enough for her to feel his warm breathing against the back of her neck.

"Get the hell away from me!"

He didn't budge.

She felt sick. Breathing was difficult. She began to choke, fighting for air.

"Melissa..."

There was concern and then fear in his voice but she put up her hand to keep him away.

"Don't...touch...me," she gasped.

She inhaled large gulps of air and exhaled at a slow rate, finally calming her rapid heartbeat.

She looked at what she was wearing, a short, red satin gown with thin spaghetti straps and matching robe. Melissa felt sick. She wanted to rip the garment from her body and throw it in the trash.

Jake liked to see her in red, often telling her the color heightened her skin tone. The woman tonight had on a bright red dress. The color made the bile in her throat roll. She'd been dozing on the bed when she heard voices.

She'd wanted to surprise him—and she did. Not realizing the surprise was on her. She inhaled long and hard, struggling for balance and turned to him, but kept her eyes averted. There would be no more tears over this man. It had hurt when Brent betrayed her, but this with Jake destroyed her. She felt as if a thousand switch-blades were slicing through her body. Would she be able to heal this time?

Melissa turned slowly toward her husband. "You're a brash, tough and unrelenting man when it comes to business. Very impatient." She nodded, lost in thought. "You have no tolerance for stupidity or mistakes. I understood that about you. It's who you are. However I saw a different side of you when it came to your family, especially Sheila. She's an important part of your life. You love her—more than anything. I said to myself... he's human. He has feelings. But above all, I felt you were an honorable man. You respected me. Protected me. I appreciated that. " She laughed without mirth. "How could I get it all wrong—again? I chose a man who doesn't give a damn. I never imagined in a million years you would deliberately set out to destroy me. Hurt me. Not you. You would never dishonor or show me such blatant disrespect. Not you," she moaned in agony. "The man with integrity." She wiped the tears that flowed. *You were an honorable man*," she sneered with disgust. "Brent—"

"Don't mention his name!"

"Go to hell!" she screamed. "Brent hurt me." She continued with defiance. "At least he had the decency to tell me to my face when it was over." She backed up. Trembling, she clenched the edges of the robe across her chest. "You'll never get the chance to hurt me again. Not ever again!"

"Will you listen? Let me explain."

"Explain what? Your lies? How many more affairs have you had?" She took deep gulps, reaching for a calm place out of her reach.

"I. Have. Never. Cheated. On. You. Please believe me."

An eerie calm settled in the room. She was drowning. As she sank deeper into the murky waters of the moment, everything floated around her mocking her distress.

"I need to make you understand...Please..." His voice was urgent and insistent.

"Who is she?" she whispered.

"No one."

"You're a liar. You called her by name so she's someone." Calmly, she asked again. "Who is she?"

Her world has falling apart, again. This time she didn't know if she would survive the devastation. With every bit of strength Melissa had, she held his gaze, waiting for an answer. He remained silent so long; she didn't believe he would answer.

She watched his shoulders rise and fall with calculated breaths.

Finally he said, "She doesn't matter."

"I'm filing for divorce."

"No," He shook his head. "It's not going to happen."

"We'll see. You have no say in this. It's over."

"I'm not letting you divorce me over a mistake. Nothing happened. We are married until death. I take our vows seriously."

The blood pounded in her ears. She wanted to scream and inflict pain.

She laughed cruelly. "Vows? You have the morals of a dog in heat."

He flinched. "Melissa—"

"Fuck you, Jake."

She ran into the bedroom and slammed the door behind her.

～

Fully dressed, Jake was stretched out on the living room sofa with one foot planted on the floor. He lay awake, with long fingers curled around the glass sitting on his chest. Now halfway through a second bottle of scotch, his body was still, eyes alert and ears keen to any sound in the suite. He wanted to be drunk but it evaded him. He only heard the tick-tock of the clock in the corner. The sound reminded him of the countdown to the gallows, informing him time was running out.

The liquor did nothing to ease the tension or erase the disgust he felt. It'd been hours since Melissa locked herself in the bedroom. He'd knocked on the door but received no answer. After a while, he turned the knob on the door and found it still locked. He'd called to her and pounded on the door.

The clock on the wall said it was three in the morning and he hadn't slept at all. He was scheduled to fly back to L.A. in two hours.

How the hell did he end up here with his marriage in shambles and hurting his wife? He felt nauseated as he remembered the hurt and sorrow etched on her face.

Her eyes had reflected it all—the sadness—the grief—the silent howl of a wounded animal.

She broke into pieces before him. It sickened him to know he was the cause of it. He'd let his pride dictate and ruin the best thing in his life. Damn. He had to fix it. But God how?

His mind drifted to the night he and Melissa had made love. Afterwards, he hated the fact that he'd succumbed. Losing himself with a woman wasn't something that happened to him but she was his Achilles heel and there was nothing he could do about it.

When he'd accused her of sleeping with her ex-husband and her slow response of denial had fueled his anger. Everything changed. Instead of backing away from her, he was drawn.

To her scent—her power—and finally her warmth.

The next morning, pissed with how easy he'd fallen under her spell and into bed, he left the house without waking her. He needed to think. To wrestle back command of his libido. The New York trip could've waited but he used it as a crutch so he wouldn't have to face her.

He hadn't wanted Bridget, but her fawning during the week had stroked his ego. A big fucking mistake! What in the hell was he thinking?

Taking a sip from the glass, he could now admit Melissa's indecisiveness between him and Sinclair hurt like hell. But it was no excuse. The look in her eyes had castrated him.

When he'd seen Melissa standing in the doorway of his bedroom in a short, red nightie, barefoot with her dark lovely hair flowing loose around her shoulders he knew she'd chosen him.

She had stood before him like a vision of feminine perfection, every man's fantasy and Jake had known at that exact moment she was all his. The untapped possessive streak rose deep within him.

Their marriage started out casual with no boundaries, Jake

mused silently, but the rules quickly changed. He loved her with every fiber of his being. She was his equal in every matter of his life.

Lying in the dark, he was forced to re-evaluate all his preconceived ideas about himself. He was shocked to discover he was actually a traditionalist when it came to marriage and commitment. He enjoyed the fact that she belonged to him. His jealousy had no merit. He had to believe that. The sudden possessiveness was so intense that he contemplated breaking down the bedroom door she was hiding behind and carrying her off to a secluded place where no man could ever look upon her again. He would never share her with anyone.

The situation was bad—real bad. Why did he let Bridget cross the threshold into his room? She meant nothing to him. Then why? To prove that a woman wanted him—and only him. It was selfish. What he did tonight proved he was as callous as people termed him. Nothing touched him. But they were wrong—Melissa touched the core of his soul.

The word divorce resonated through his mind. When she said the word, he saw the moment she'd let go. A peaceful calm came over her face.

The tears stopped.

The screaming stopped.

The silent howl stopped.

She had given up. But he hadn't. He couldn't. Failure wasn't an option.

He rubbed at the discomfort in his eyes. He sighed deeply and slowly his eyes drifted shut.

Just for a moment he needed to breathe—to rest.

He awoke with a start, startled. He sat straight up. His foot hit an empty whiskey bottle and glass beside the sofa. He squeezed his eyes tight, praying the room would stop spinning. Why was he on the couch? He looked around the room, stood slowly, hindered by the headache, and moved to the bedroom. Then he remembered. Melissa. Last night's horrible events hit him, causing him to stumble in his wake.

The doors to the bedroom stood wide open. He rushed through. There was no sign of his wife. The bed hadn't been slept in but the comforter showed a slight indication, which meant she'd at least lain across the bed. He flung open the closet doors. They were empty. He looked around the room to see if there were any other signs of her presence, a piece of clothing, a hairbrush. There was none.

He grabbed the phone on the nightstand and punched in some numbers. When the person picked up, he said curtly, "What time did my wife leave?"

He didn't identify himself, knowing that the penthouse suite number showed on the caller ID.

"Pardon me, sir?" The person at the front desk stumbled over his words.

"My wife. I know she had to come through the lobby."

"Sir, we only have you registered in the suite. I really don't—"

"Dammit. I don't want to hear about rules or regulations. Someone in the hotel had to bring my wife to my suite. I don't care who the hell it was. Right now, I want to know if you or someone else called a cab for her this morning."

The man cleared his throat. "I— believe—"

Jake's hand tightened around the phone handle. "Speak up, man. I don't have all day."

"Ah…Yes sir. I called the cab."

"How long ago?" The wall clock showed it was four-thirty a.m. He had slept for a little over an hour. Damn.

"Thirty minutes ago."

He severed the connection and punched in his pilot's number. "Ready the plane. We take off in twenty minutes.

CHAPTER ELEVEN

Jake rang the doorbell and waited. After a few seconds he pushed the button again. Finally the door opened.

"Mr. Sorensen?" A heavyset Hispanic woman dressed in a black and white uniform observed him with an expressionless stare.

"Is my cousin home?" he asked gruffly.

"Yes, sir." She stepped back to let him proceed over the threshold. "Please follow me."

They walked through the long corridor. Coming upon a large, open glass door, he stepped through to the patio outside. His cousin sat on a white, cushioned chair with her feet propped on another chair. A magazine was open across her pregnant belly. Her head was thrown back with a hand across her eyes, shielding them from the sun. She didn't appear to be asleep, but enjoying the late afternoon sun.

"Sheila."

The magazine fell to the marble floor of the patio. Jake reached to retrieve it and place it on the glass table beside her.

"Jake?"

"I didn't mean to startle you."

"What are you doing here? I thought you were in New York." She looked behind him. "Where's Melissa?"

Wearily, he ran a hand through his hair and looked out over the massive backyard lawn toward the horizon where the brilliant sun had boldly retreated, leaving him without warmth.

He and Sheila were born into wealth. Although he was four years older, they'd been kindred spirits since childhood. Always determined to forge their own paths in life without the help of the family money. She became a successful attorney, moving up to become the lead prosecutor in the state of California. While he started his business with bank loans, refusing to touch the two large trust funds left to him by his maternal and paternal grandparents.

He was an only child who grew up with a stern father but a good man. His loving mother had died during his last year of college from cancer. She'd always been his fiercest champion, encouraging him to make his own way in the world. He hadn't wanted to join the family business. With his father's disapproval and his mother's encouragement, he followed his dream and created his own business. She never lived to see his success. Her death changed him. He became insolent, angry and the man he was today—afraid of letting anyone see his weaknesses.

Sheila's mother had left her father for another man when she was ten. Sheila had only seen her twice in the twenty years since. With two older brothers and a father who treated her like she was fragile, she'd refused to be what her father and brothers wanted, a pampered, rich princess so she became tough, strong-willed and rebellious.

Four generations old, the family business was still run by their fathers and her brothers.

"I asked you a question, Jake."

"I don't know where Melissa is," he snapped.

She swung her feet over the side and stood. "What do mean, you don't know? I specifically helped her pack and dropped her off at the airport."

"Have you heard from her?" Jake asked.

"No, I haven't."

He observed her face. "Where would she go if she was upset?"

Her eyes narrowed. "What did you do?"

"What makes you think I did something?"

"Because I know you like the back of my hand. Damn, Jake. I encouraged her to surprise you. Tell me you didn't reject her?"

"It's complicated."

"What happened?"

He pinched the edge of his nose and squeezed his eyes against the headache he couldn't seem to shake. He was tense and damn tired. He arrived in L.A. a few hours ago and headed straight to his house. Not finding his wife in residence, he left and went to the office. She wasn't there either and her assistant hadn't heard from her. He even went to the condo she had lived in before their marriage and still owned. There was no sign she had been there either. Everything was still covered in furniture canvas from when she moved out three months ago.

Jake rubbed the tension at his temple. "Why didn't you call to let me know she was coming?"

"Duh. You do know the definition of a surprise, don't you?"

"Damn, Sheila. I didn't know Melissa was in the penthouse suite when I walked in."

"Jake. Stop stalling. Spit it out."

"I had a woman there."

Sheila poked him in his chest. She sputtered and went to do it again.

"Stop, Sheila." He grabbed her hand and then let her go. "You haven't poked me that hard since you were eleven." He rubbed the sore spot.

"You asshole! You know her ex-husband destroyed her confidence when he told her he was in love with another woman. Now you go and cut the wound wide open again. Why in the hell did you marry her if you couldn't keep your dick in your pants? Melissa's nothing like those bimbos you dated in the past."

"It was a mistake. Nothing happened with the woman. I've never cheated on Melissa," he interjected.

"Bullshit. You wouldn't bring a woman to your suite without screwing her."

"Will you curb that acid tongue of yours? I didn't screw anyone."

"Then why?"

"Bridget was a—"

She raised her hand. "Stop. You knew the woman?" she said, incredulously.

"Yes."

She rolled her eyes. "How could you, Jake? Never mind. Don't answer. I know the answer. You needed to prove your dick could still get hard for someone else."

Jake flushed darkly, not liking the way that sounded, but slowed his anger. Sheila knew more about his past association with women than anyone.

"I'm telling you nothing happened. Damn. I've done a lot of inexcusable things in my lifetime, but I couldn't go through with it." He was silent for a long moment. The only sound was the warm wind swaying through the trees on the property. "I love her, Sheila."

She sighed deeply. "I know you do, but damn if you don't have a funny way of showing it. You messed up big time."

"How do I fix it?"

He wasn't surprised his voice cracked on the words. Vulnerability wasn't something he was used to.

"I don't know. You let your pride, ego and Melissa's ex-husband throw you into a cesspool."

"Sinclair has nothing to do with it."

"Don't lie to me, Jake Sorensen! You were afraid Melissa was going back to Brent Sinclair. You decided to cover all bases and beat her to home plate."

"Damn, Sheila. You always go for the jugular. I've made a mess of my marriage. I don't need you to keep throwing gas on the fire. It's already a blaze." He rubbed his jaw to loosen the tightness. He hadn't realized he had been clenching his teeth. "I need your help on this."

"You're destructive, Jake. Melissa is the best thing that ever happened to you."

He inhaled deeply and released it. "I know."

"You changed when your mom died. You're a hard man and can be a cold son-of-a-bitch. Now you're letting it destroy your marriage."

"You have a nasty mouth. When did you start cursing so much?"

"You forget I grew up with only men in the house."

He almost smiled.

"She's running, Sheila. The only road block I have is to deny her the divorce."

Her eyes widened with shock. "What? A divorce? Damn. Damn. This is bad! If she asked for a divorce, she's given up on the marriage...and you."

"Melissa didn't ask for the divorce. She said she was divorcing me. There is a difference."

"You're grasping at straws."

"I'm desperate. I need you to talk to her...Please."

"You are my cousin. She's my best friend. I'm not going to take sides."

"Will you call her?"

"Damn. Jake, don't put me in the middle of this."

"I'm desperate, Sheila."

"I won't call her because she'll know I'm calling to talk about you. But, if she calls me, I'll try your case."

"Okay. At this point, I'm grateful for what I can get."

"You need to make the first move toward her."

"How can I when she won't answer any of my texts or calls?"

"This is major. Real serious shit. You need to be careful and figure out how you're going to get her back."

"I must *find* her."

"She's wounded, Jake. Give her some time."

"I can't. I'm afraid I'll lose her."

"That's a chance you may have to take."

Chapter Twelve

Jake slammed his hands on the desk, knocking over the glass paperweight. His usual self-control had been distinctly lacking in the last few months.

"What the fuck am I paying you for? It's been two months. You haven't given me anything substantial."

Jake stood and came around the desk. Cold, hard logic told him he was dealing with men who couldn't begin to understand his wife's way of thinking. If she wanted to disappear, she would. He glared at the two private investigators. Right now he was pissed and frustrated. His entire life was unraveling and he couldn't stop it. These men were supposed to be the best but at the moment he doubted it.

His friend, Matthew Connor sat quietly slouched in a chair nearby not saying anything but watched him as he ranted at the men. Every now and then Matthew frowned at him. That was his cue to calm down but it wasn't working.

The older of the private investigators cleared his throat nervously. "Mr. Sorensen there is something. On the morning you left New York, your wife didn't. She went into a bank and withdrew five thousand dollars from her personal account. She has been paying for everything with cash. There's no record of her using credit cards. If she had, it would definitely have left a trail. The problem is cash doesn't...ah, in most cases, that is."

Blasted out of his usual cool by that less than helpful statement, he said, "Is that all?" His voice filled with anger. "If it is, then you haven't given me a damn thing. You're supposed to be the best. At the moment, I don't see any evidence of it."

On the receiving end of his icy tone, a red tinge skimmed the investigator's faces. The one that had been speaking cleared his throat again and peered at his silent partner seated beside him.

"Huh...there was a spotting of her in Vermont a week after you left New York, but it couldn't be verified."

"That was two months ago. What else do you have?" Jake asked.

The man glanced at his notes in his lap and paused before looking at Jake. "She was also seen in Miami. A woman renting a small cottage on Star Island matched her description. I have dispensed my men to Florida to investigate."

"How long ago was this?" Jake asked.

"Ah...three days ago."

Jake walked to the front door of his home and opened it. "Find her," he said in a soft, lethal voice that had the men hurrying to the door. "Hire more men. I want every state in the union searched. I want people at airports, trains and bus stations. None of your men rest until her whereabouts are discovered. I want a report within twenty-four hours."

The men scurried out and he slammed the door behind them.

"Imbeciles," he murmured and started to pace, knowing that his anxiety levels were high due to the fact that, as each day passed, the chance of finding her was getting slimmer.

He picked up the phone and dialed his pilot. "File a flight plan for Miami. I want to leave within the hour."

"Jake—"

"I know, Matt." He rubbed his eyes and started to pace. Sleep wasn't something he was getting enough of lately. He was lucky to get a couple of hours a night. His work was suffering. He looked like hell but he didn't care. Finding Melissa was top priority. "I really fucked up." He stopped pacing, looked through the large bay window and then turned to his friend. "I'm paying for it. I'm her husband, damnit. She's hiding from me."

"I know," Matthew said. "But you can't keep flying off the handle at every disappointment. Going to Miami won't help the situation. You hired the investigators, let them do their job."

Emotions unknown gripped him. Never in his life did he feel the need to explain his actions to anyone and yet suddenly he was filled with a burning need to locate his wife and explain every tiny detail of his missteps.

He had hurt her and in the process hurt himself. Frustration and concern mingled when a severe attack of conscience hit him.

"For two months, I've sat back and let them do just that. Today's information was like real time. Three days ago in Miami...I've been given a lifeline. I have friends who live on Star Island. I may be able to get some information about her."

Surprise showed on Matthew's face. "You're going to expose the fact your wife left you? What happened to the ultra-private Jake Sorensen I know? Damn. You wouldn't even give an interview to Forbes Magazine."

Jake frowned. "I don't give a fuck what I expose. If there is a chance in hell I can get her back, I'm taking it."

Jake reached for the divorce papers lying on the table and tore them into pieces. "I'm not giving her a divorce. Somewhere in the last two months, she slipped into L.A. to file the papers. I contacted her lawyer but she wouldn't talk. I was given some bullshit about attorney client privileges. No matter how nice I was—"

"You...nice?"

"To the best of my ability. I was downright submissive. The lawyer was a barracuda. "

Matt laughed. "That's a compliment coming from you. I would've loved to see you grovel. Melissa's attorney is right, you know. She could've been disbarred if she gave you information on her client."

"I don't give a damn. I told her I want a meeting face to face with Melissa, until then, I'm not signing shit."

"Jake, you're being difficult. It's not going to help. Not in this situation. Melissa doesn't kneel to threats. She can be as stubborn as you."

"It's my only weapon."

"How long are you going to fight the divorce?"

"Forever if I have to."

"The possibility of you finding her gets slimmer as each day passes. You might never find her. You need to reconcile yourself to that fact." Matthew's tone was solemn.

"That's not an option I'll entertain." His voice was devoid of emotion. "*I will find her.*" The words came without hesitation.

CHAPTER THIRTEEN

Melissa slid into the back seat of the chauffeured SUV and rested her eyes. She was exhausted. For the past two months, she'd zigzagged across the United States, not staying long in one spot.

Jake betrayed her. The memory of what transpired that night in his hotel room was still fresh. She inhaled deeply, waiting for the ache to subside. It didn't. The hollowness still held her in its grip. Thinking about Jake caused such ravaging pain in her chest she couldn't breathe.

Was fool stamped on her forehead? Why was she drawn to men who couldn't or wouldn't commit?

After checking into a modest hotel in New York, she'd stayed in the city for two days, hiding from Jake. She knew he would immediately think she'd returned to L.A.

When she left New York, she went to Vermont, stayed in a cozy cabin sat in the window seat and watched the snow fall. Then she flew into Los Angeles long enough to file the divorce papers and leave. A few weeks ago, she landed in Miami and rented a small beach house. She found she liked the city with its hustle and bright nightlife, beaches and sunshine

Being in Miami gave her time to reflect, especially about her parents. She hadn't spoken to them in five years. Whenever she did think about them, she pushed the thoughts away. Examining the pros and cons, she decided it was time she confronted the demons of her past.

An hour ago, she'd landed in Dallas, where it all began.

The car slowed when the driver turned onto a long road leading to her parent's palatial estate. Melissa looked out the window at the passing scenery and felt an array of emotions—sadness—fear, joy and rejection.

This was the place where she grew up and loved—and hated. When she left Dallas, she'd left everything behind—memories, good and bad—and her parents.

For a moment, the thought of leaving consumed her. Finally she took a deep breath, her l heart still racing, she squared her shoulders and stepped out. She stood beside the car and observed the familiar grounds; four hundred acres of prime Texas real estate. There were over two thousand trees on the property.

She remembered her mother stating if Oprah Winfrey could have that many trees on her property, so could she.

Many rose bushes, several displaying different colored buds, flanked the front of the house, giving it a very rich and whimsical atmosphere.

The house itself was a statement. It was an impressive 10,000 square-foot mansion. With seven bedrooms and six and a half baths, it was featured in *Architectural Digest* two years straight. No one would ever say her mother wasn't pretentious. She wore it like a crown of glory.

She turned and spoke to the driver. "I don't know how long I'll be. I'll call when I'm ready to leave this place."

He nodded. "Yes, ma'am."

He got into the SUV and left. Melissa watched the vehicle until it was out of sight.

She rang the doorbell. The door was immediately opened as if she had been expected.

"Oh, my Lord," the tall gray-haired woman said, a hand flying to her chest. Her dark brown face was weathered but still strong. She hadn't changed much since Melissa last saw her. Only her hair showed whiter than she remembered. The woman's eyes filled with tears. "Missy? I can't believe it's you. You've come home to me."

"Hello, Miss Sarah." Melissa offered a genuine smile at the nickname only Sarah called her. Her mother hated the name, which only caused her to love it more. She stepped through the doorway into the huge foyer.

It never sat well with her mother that she called a member of the staff "miss." She'd told her many times it wasn't proper etiquette and not done in their social circle. But Melissa had stuck to her guns, giving the old woman the respect due to an elder well advanced in age.

She grabbed Melissa in a big hug, squeezing so hard she struggled for air. Melissa eased away so she could breathe, but Sarah held her hands. This lady had been with the family since well before she was born.

She'd treated her like a cherished granddaughter. Sarah had been there during her childhood, teenage years, giving her an abundance of love and support, something she never received from her own parents. More importantly, she'd been a rock to lean on when her marriage to Brent was ending. She felt remorse she hadn't kept in touch with the older woman but, at the time, it'd been too hard.

Melissa continued to smile. "It's good to see you."

"You don't know how much you've made this old woman happy today." She took a clean white handkerchief from the pocket of her apron and wiped her eyes.

"I'm glad."

"Come on in, child." She pulled Melissa through the door. "You must be weary."

"I'm fine. Are my parents at home?"

"They're havin' afternoon tea in the drawing room."

Melissa glanced at her watch. "It's a little late for that, isn't it?"

Sarah laughed heartily. "Indeed it is. But Mr. Delaney was late comin' in from his golf game. You know your mama, she likes tradition."

Melissa frowned. "How well I know."

An uncomfortable silence followed.

The housekeeper cleared her throat. "Come on, let me walk you back."

"No need. I remember where it is."

"Of course you do, honey." She patted Melissa's hand. "I'm just so glad to see ya. I'm beside myself. I'll just go and finish fixin' the supper."

Melissa patted her hand. "I'll see you before I leave."

Sarah's eyes widened. "Leave? You ain't staying?"

"No, I'm not."

"Well, at least stay for a bite to eat. We're having rosemary-roasted chicken and a big old T-bone steak for your daddy."

Melissa smiled. "I'm surprised Mother hasn't made Daddy give up red meat."

Sarah chuckled. "She tried, honey. But, Mr. Delaney, being a true Texan, put his foot down on that one."

"And mother caved in?"

"Not without a fight. But your daddy held his ground."

"Things have changed."

"In some ways," she said softly. "Missy, I promise I'll prepare one of your favorites to go along with supper. Glazed carrots with sweet cream butter, cinnamon sticks, vanilla bean and fresh basil," she said, eagerly. "How's that sound?"

"Oh, Miss Sarah. It sounds wonderful. I haven't had that since I left Dallas. But, I can't promise I'll stay.

Sadness showed on the old lady's face.

Contrite, Melissa said, "Why don't you fix me a small container to go?"

A bright smile broke out on Sarah, creating creases around her mouth. "Okay. Now go on, so I can get done."

Melissa laughed, kissed her on the check and walked the rest of the way through the foyer. When she reached the double doors, the voices of her parents were low, but she heard clearly her mother chastising her father for delaying their afternoon tea. As usual he said nothing. He hated tea but did anything to appease her mother.

She entered through the opened door unnoticed. The elegant décor, although different from the last time she was in the room, still conveyed the flavor of an English countryside mansion. No one could say her mother didn't have style or class.

"Hello," she said, softly.

Both parents looked toward the door, shock riveted on their faces. No one moved as they looked at each other in silence. She walked toward them. Her father was the first to come out of his stupor and rose to his feet. He met her halfway and engulfed her into his arms.

"Oh my God, Melissa!" He murmured her name over and over again. She squeezed her eyes, holding back the tears, savoring the peace and warmth of being in her father's arms. No matter what had happened in the past, she loved him unconditionally. She realized at that moment how much she'd missed him.

She tried to pull back but he held her closer and she let him. Finally, he loosened his grip and created a small space between them. Tears in his eyes escaped down his cheeks.

She swallowed hard. "Hi Daddy," she said, breathlessly. "It's good to see you."

"You too, honey."

Jasper John Delaney was a handsome man. Golfing, horseback riding and those ski trips to Aspen every winter kept his tall frame lean through the years. At fifty-eight, his blond-hair showed speckles of gray throughout but it didn't take anything away from him. He was the same man she had idolized from afar all of her life.

He pulled back. "Let me take a good look at you."

She tried not to squirm as he examined her.

"You're still my beautiful baby girl."

She smiled. "I'm no longer a baby or a girl, Daddy."

"You'll always be my baby." He put his arm around her and walked with her toward her mother. "Elizabeth, our girl has come home."

Her mother remained seated. "I see." Her tone held no welcome. She looked her up and down without expression. "It's good you kept your weight off. You have a tendency to fluctuate between five to ten pounds."

"Elizabeth!" Her father's voice ricocheted throughout the room. "You haven't seen our daughter in five years. Is that all you can do is to make a disparaging remark about her weight?"

Melissa flinched when her mother's features tightened into a hard mask. She backed up a step. But her father held her steady and rubbed her arm with a reassuring gesture. After all of these years, Elizabeth Delaney still had the ability to wound her. She took a deep breath, determined not to let her mother see how much her words hurt her.

She'd built up confidence through the years and she would be damned if she'd let her mother destroy it.

"What the hell has gotten into you woman?" Her father continued his tone, now cold and forbidding. "I know you can be snobbish, abrupt and a borderline bitch, but I've never known you to be cruel, especially to your own child."

"Daddy!"

Melissa was shocked. She'd never heard her father talk like that to her mother.

Her mother's very light skin paled at her father's reprimand. Her lips pursed tightly together, creating wrinkles around her mouth. She glared at her husband and then at her, rose slowly from her chair, and smoothed down her silk Carolina Herrera dress.

She folded her hands together and remained erect. She stood poised as if she was getting ready to deliver an important speech to a large stadium of people.

"What's *gotten* into you, Jasper to make you think you can speak to me like that? I won't tolerate it."

Her father released Melissa and now stood facing her mother. "You won't tolerate?" He laughed humorlessly. "I have tolerated more than any man when it comes to you. I stood on the sidelines and watched you isolate our daughter from this family. When she married Brent you were finally a mother, not great, but *decent*, which isn't saying a lot. But that didn't last long."

"Daddy! Don't."

"No, baby, this needs to be said."

"If you stood back and watched, what does that say about you?" Elizabeth said sarcastically.

"I admit I was a shitty father. When it came to you, I had no backbone—"

"And you have some now?" she sneered. "Do you want me to offer congratulations?"

"Stop it! Both of you. I didn't come back to tear you apart—"

"Then why did you come!" Her mother's frigid tone caused her to catch her breath.

A chill ran the length of her spine. Melissa wouldn't back down now. She couldn't. This was too important. "Why do you hate me so much?"

Elizabeth gasped. Her eyes quickly widened with hurt but it disappeared as quickly as it came. She was now the mistress of her emotions. Melissa felt her eyes were playing tricks on her. Pain was what her mother gave other people, not something she felt.

"What are you talking about?" Elizabeth asked.

She heard surprise in those curt words. This proud woman, whom she'd always tried to please and couldn't, looked confused at her words.

"You heard me, Mother. All my life I've tried to be exactly what you wanted—studious—accommodating—and appreciative to be the daughter of Elizabeth and Jasper Delaney. But it was never enough for you."

Elizabeth blinked as if she was in a fog. She shook her head in bewilderment. "I've always wanted what was best for you."

"No, *you wanted* what was best for you—your image—your house, and your friends. Those were the important things in your life."

Helplessly she looked at her husband. "Jasper... Are you going to let your daughter talk to me like that?"

Her father didn't say a word. Elizabeth Delaney took a long and deep breath, her hand going to the genuine fresh-water pearls at her neck. In a quick movement she twisted them through her manicured fingers.

"I don't need Daddy to fight my battles, Mother. I stopped scratching and digging for the crumbs you carelessly drop along the way a *long* time ago."

Her mother flinched but ironically it didn't faze Melissa. She was tired of being the one who begged for acceptance. If her own mother never loved her. She now accepted it. She'd lost too much in her life, Brent, their friendship, and Jake. Distress gripped her as her mind skimmed on the last encounter with her husband. She shook her head. No more dwelling on what could've been. It was over.

"How dare you? I'm your mother."

"Since when?" she countered, sarcastically.

"Watch your tone, young lady," her father admonished.

"I'm sorry, Daddy."

"Don't say it to me, say it to your mother."

The silence stretched. Finally, she said in a low voice, "I apologize." She couldn't manage to direct the apology to her mother so it fell between them like a dead weight of nothing.

She knew better, but it seemed as if a driving force was pushing for her to confront the past.

"It's not always about what you feel or think, Melissa. There are things you don't know."

She wanted to shout at her whose fault was that, but didn't. The atmosphere in the room was already toxic. There was no need to add to it.

Her mother came to stand in front of her. "I didn't know you had so much animosity toward me, Melissa. I may not have been the typical mother but I was the best I could be." Elizabeth twisted her hands and then pointed to the love seat. "Take a seat."

She didn't move at the command.

"Please."

Melisa thought maybe she should stick her finger in her ear to make sure it wasn't clogged. Did she just hear Elizabeth Delaney say please? She walked to the sofa and took a seat. Her mother sat beside her but didn't touch her. Melissa glanced at her father for direction. He threw her a smile, a quick wink of encouragement and moved to a chair across from them but near enough for her to reach out and touch him. He slid into it and stretched out his long legs.

Her mother took a deep breath and folded her hands onto her lap. "From the moment I found out I was pregnant, it scared the hell out me."

Melissa eyes widened. She'd never heard her mother use a curse word in her life. Times had changed.

"You see, you weren't planned. To be frank, I didn't want a child. But your father..." She cast a glance at her husband and then back at her. "He was elated. I kept thinking, a baby? What would I do with it? It was too much. The disruption to our lives would be massive. A child was a lifetime commitment. I didn't want it."

"Wow, you didn't want me," Melissa said snidely. "That's not a new revelation. I've known all my life that I wasn't wanted. Sorry to disappoint you, Mother."

"I'm trying to explain some things to you but I won't tolerate your sarcasm."

She laughed harshly. "You *won't* tolerate? I've tolerated more than enough from you that would last me a lifetime."

A puzzled frown rested on her mother's face "What are you talking about?"

"You wanted a very light skinned baby but got a chocolate one."

Elizabeth's eyes widened with confusion. "That's ridiculous."

"Is it? I doubt it. All my life you made me feel inferior because of my skin tone. You were always telling me to smooth out the dark spots. Use the creams you bought for me. Don't pucker my lips because they were already large enough. Stay out of the sun. I got your message loud and clear."

"That's not true. You've misinterpreted everything. I was trying to help you."

"Help me? How?"

"You're the product of a mixed marriage. I didn't want you to go through the trauma I did. I wanted...you to...be happy." Elizabeth looked at her husband helplessly." Jasper..."

Her father sat on the edge of his seat now with his hands dangling between his legs. Finally he folded them and directed his gaze to Melissa. "Baby girl, I know you can't believe that nonsense. Your mother is a little eccentric but not prejudiced against her own daughter."

"Daddy, you're wrong. I came back here to confront old hurts and ghosts. Everything I did in the past five years was done to prove to myself that I was good enough. In L.A., I found a job based on my degree. I was given a chance to learn, to build and move up in the company on my own merits. I was no longer the dark child not wanted."

"Melissa, you're talking foolishness." Elizabeth glared at her. "I won't stand for you making me a villain in this. Your decisions and feelings were all yours. I didn't do or say anything to warrant these accusations."

"You don't get it, do you?" Melissa laughed mercilessly. "You're not perfect. I loved Brent but I married him because I knew it would make you happy. But I also wanted someone to love me. Foolishly, I thought he did."

"I'm not going to accept blame me for your failures." Her mother turned to her father. "Are you going to let her continue this tirade?"

"She's telling us what she felt, Lizzie. We just can't dismiss it. Our daughter was hurting and we didn't see it. We've done enough damage. It's time to make it right."

Elizabeth huffed. "Well, I have never been so insulted—"

"This isn't about you, darling. For once, put yourself in Melissa's shoes. She didn't ask to be born. We chose to bring her into this world." He took his wife hands in his. "All she asked was to be loved—by the both of us. We failed her. " He kissed her hands and gave them a gentle pat. "Help her to understand. Talk to her."

Melissa watched fear cloud her mother's eyes. What was wrong with her? She acted as if she was afraid to talk to her.

"I gave birth to you. I'm not prejudiced against my own child."

"Tell her all of it, Lizzie," Jasper urged. "It's about time we let our daughter into our lives."

Melissa snuck a peek at her mother. She knew she hated being called Lizzie but somehow never objected when her father used it.

"It's not easy."

Melissa glanced at both of her parents. "I didn't come to disrupt your lives, but I need answers."

Her father pulled his chair next to her mother. He touched her arm, giving it a slow loving rub. "Take your time, my love."

Elizabeth took a deep breath. There was a strained silence as she eyed her husband and her daughter. At that moment she seemed vulnerable. It was strange to see her mother nervous and unsure of herself.

She took another breath and directed her words to Melissa. "You know I had an older brother, Ethan, who was killed in Vietnam during the last weeks of the war. What you don't know is that his death destroyed my mother. She died three months after his death. Mama had health problems, arthritis, recurring sinus infections, but nothing that would've caused her to die."

She fingered the pearls at her neck again. Melissa stared at her. Realizing the nervous gesture, her mother removed her hands and folded them in her lap.

"Ethan was only 19 years old. It was such a waste of a bright young man with a promising future. I was 13 at the time."

"You never discussed him. I just assumed you were estranged from him at the time of his death," Melissa uttered softly

"It has always been hard for me to talk about him. He was my world...my knight. I was devastated by his death. Mother was consumed by grief and my father grew silent and withdrawn. I had no one to talk to about what I was feeling. I became a very angry and rebellious teenager. Ethan treated me like a princess. I loved him. Along with my father, he was my hero."

Elizabeth dropped her head, took another deep breath and lifted it again. "I vowed never to love like that again. I surmised that it only caused heartache. I witnessed it first-hand. My father never recovered from mama's death. His Irish, American wealthy family had disowned him when he married a black woman," she laughed cruelly. "Although my mother was mixed with Irish and Native American blood, it was the portion of black blood she carried that mattered the most. It was the 1950's. An interracial marriage was unacceptable and, in some states, against the law, Texas being one of them. It was hard for them and for my brother and me."

"You're light enough to pass for white," Melissa said.

"I know. I'm ashamed to say that sometimes I pretended to be white. It made life a little easier. When my father found out he was disappointed. Although the world saw me as black, Papa told me I was a mixture of pureness. A product of him and mama's love. I was ashamed. I loved my mother and knew she was proud of her heritage."

"I didn't know your grandmother, baby girl, but I knew your grandfather. He was a proud man," Jasper interjected.

My mother nodded. "My father never remarried and cherished my mother until death. I want you to understand where I come from. It's something I should've shared with you. I didn't think it was important but I was wrong. Because of the threats on their lives, my parents moved to Europe after the birth of my brother. I was born there. Papa made a fortune in agriculture machinery and moved back to Texas in 1970. It was a new era but bigotry was still strong. Having money caused some good ole Texans to ignore the fact that my father had a wife and children who were black. It made me tough. I felt loving someone would break your heart and destroy you."

Melissa frowned. "But you loved Daddy, didn't you?"

Her eyes softened with a smile when she looked at her husband. "I love your father very much, but I didn't at first."

"What—" Shock riveted in her voice.

"He knows."

Jasper Delaney cleared his throat and said, "Sweetheart, from the moment I saw your mama walking across Texas Southern University campus, I knew she would be my wife. I was a second year graduate student and she was there visiting a friend. I didn't know at the time she was a sophomore at University of LaVerne in California. But it didn't matter. I would've gone to the ends of the earth to make her mine. It didn't matter that she didn't feel the same as I did. I had enough love for the both of us."

"Jasper was a very handsome, charismatic and confident man." She laughed softly. "He was determined to have me and I was just as determined not to be caught. Every time I turned around on my campus, he was there with flowers, chocolates, and good old-fashioned courtship. I was in awe of him." She looked deeply into his eyes. "I still am. He was my first and only lover."

There it was. That all-consuming love she witnessed between her parents. She was always the outsider looking in and never invited to join in the celebration of their love. Funny how now after all of these years, she understood it.

Melissa waited for the agony to claim her. It was only a prick this time. Something she could withstand. She'd finally grown into her own self-worth. It'd been a struggle but she made it.

"I felt like I didn't belong in your lives," Melissa said.

Her mother leaned toward her and laid her hand on hers. Melissa was stunned. Her mother never touched anyone unless it was her father. To feel her skin, fleeting as it was, against hers was almost her undoing. She didn't move, afraid the slim connection would be broken. She inhaled, absorbing the fragrance of Cuir d'Ange, the French perfume her mother had worn for years.

"I don't know how to be a good mother." Elizabeth Delaney said matter-of-factly. "I've never been something that others wanted me to be. I am who I am. I don't think I can change."

"You haven't tried, Lizzie," her father said. "This is our daughter we're talking about. I know you want a relationship with her. I know you love her."

"Don't speak for me," she said, curtly.

He laughed heartily and didn't seem to be perturbed by her harsh tone. "Oh, believe me. I wouldn't *dare* speak for you, my love. But I *do* know you. Better than you know yourself. I love you as much or even more than the day I married you. I know deep-down you love our daughter. Since she's been gone, I've seen the disappointment in your eyes as months, years and holidays passed and she never called or came to visit. Five years is a long time to pretend that everything is right in your world."

"You don't know everything, Jasper."

He just smiled at her. "Take down the wall you've put up between the two of you. Our daughter has come home. It's time to start fresh."

Melissa opened her mouth and exhaled soundlessly. Tears formed in her eyes and rolled down her cheeks.

Elizabeth removed her hand from hers. "I'm not an easy person. I can't get back the years lost." She paused. "But we can try at least to open the lines of communication."

Melissa was so overwhelmed she couldn't speak but managed to nod her acceptance.

"Well, that's a beginning," her father said, "I have something to say to you, baby girl. I was so afraid of losing your mother that I cut my own daughter out of my life. I didn't do it intentionally but it happened all the same."

"I forgive you, Daddy."

She heard her mother's swift intake. It was easier to forgive her father but she and her mother had a long road to travel. It wouldn't be easy but she was at least willing to try.

"I have grown up a lot in the last five years. I survived. I had no choice."

"It hurts that we weren't there for you, baby." Jasper's voice was filled with hurt.

"If you don't mind me asking," her mother said, "where were you?"

"California."

"So far but yet so near." Jasper stood to his feet. Melissa and her mother stood also, looking at him. "Stay for a while, baby girl."

"I...don't—" she started.

"We want you to stay don't we, Lizzie?" he asked his wife.

Her mother was quiet so long that Melissa didn't think she would respond to her father's question.

Elizabeth frowned at Jasper, threw Melissa a quick glance. "Stay."

Her father released a long sigh. Just one word, Melissa thought, was all that her mother could manage. She sighed and shook her head. Elizabeth Delaney wasn't a woman who liked to be cornered. Although she said stay, it wasn't personal. Melissa wasn't looking for her to change but she would at least try to have some sort of relationship. After all these years, she found it sobering that she still needed, or rather wanted, to connect with her.

"Alright. But only until tomorrow."

"It's been five years, baby girl, I want more than tomorrow."

"I don't have any clothes with me."

Jasper reached over, touched her arm and then stepped back. "You know that's not a problem. We can have your mother's stylist come to the house, take your measurements and buy everything you need."

"Daddy, that's not necessary. I can go shopping."

"Nonsense. We want to do this, don't we Lizzie?"

Sarah came quietly in the room. "Dinner is served, Mrs. Delaney."

Luckily, her mother was saved from answering yet another question. She sighed. A relationship took time to build. Hopefully, she and her mother would get to the point in the road where they could start the journey and not end up at a dead end.

Melissa squinted at Sarah and noticed the old woman's eyes were bright. She hid a smile when she realized Sarah must've been listening outside the door. Times hadn't changed that much.

"Thank you, Sarah," her mother said.

Jasper offered an arm to his wife and daughter. "It would be my pleasure to escort my favorite two ladies into dinner."

They each took an arm and walked toward the dining room.

Chapter Fourteen

The days turned into weeks and Melissa learned a lot about her parents. It started off strange, new, and then comfortable. She came to realize her father processed a wicked sense of humor. Her mother laughed at his jokes, even though they weren't funny. Her parents talked a lot, bickered, or rather her mother did, and constantly touched each other. It was as if they couldn't help themselves. They were in their own little world. It was amazing to watch, but Melissa noticed her father always managed to include her in their conversations. Elizabeth Delaney sometimes looked at her with confusion. Melissa honestly didn't believe her mother knew what to say to her. But she was trying. Melissa didn't ask or expect more.

They went shopping, took long walks around the property, which she felt made her mother uncomfortable, so she did most of the talking.

Then one day after being home for a month, she and her mother had lunch at a little French restaurant tucked in a secluded hideaway on the outskirts of Dallas. The food was delicious and the atmosphere authentically 16th century French. Deciding she wasn't going to carry the conversation, she asked questions about things she knew her mother would be interested in. Before she realized it they had talked, with her mother participating, for over two hours. It was the first break toward communicating with each other. It felt good.

In the evenings, they would retire to the library for more conversation.

Curled on a sofa with her feet tucked beneath her thighs, she sipped on a cup of herbal tea, while her parents played bridge. She could never grasp the card game. It was too slow for her peace of mind.

She took another sip of the tea. "It's so peaceful here."

Her father chuckled. "Yelp. Real quiet except for the crickets." He spread his cards on the table.

Elizabeth frowned. "Jasper, you cheated."

"Honey, you always say that when you lose."

Her mother stood. "I'm going to ring for fresh tea. Does anyone want anything?"

"Mother," Melissa pointed to the ceramic carafe on the high end table. "My pot is still hot. You're welcome to share."

Elizabeth hesitated a moment. She poured a cup and sat beside Melissa on the long sofa.

"Thanks." She took a sip. "You're right. It's still hot."

Jasper retrieved his sniffer glass from the table and took a chair in front of them. "Melissa, you've been here a month. I must say it's good to have you home. I wish you would stay indefinitely." He threw her a sly grin and sipped on his drink.

"I know what you're doing, Daddy, and it's not going to work."

"Well, you can't blame your old man for trying."

"I hope you stay, Melissa. I like having you here," her mother said, nonchalantly as she placed her cup on the coffee table and straightened a magazine that didn't need it.

A strong silence fell in the room. Jasper and she stared at her in shock.

She looked up and caught them staring. "What?" she asked. Confusion lined her face.

"Honey, you said you wanted Melissa to stay and that you liked having her here."

She frowned. "So?"

Jasper laughed, shook his head and patted Melissa's hand. "See what I mean, baby girl, your mama is a complicated woman."

"I have no idea what you're trying to say, Jasper Delaney, but there better be a compliment in there somewhere."

His booming laughter saturated the room. "There is, honey. Believe me there is."

Her mother looked at her. "Do you have any idea what your father is talking about?"

Melissa sat up and swung her bare feet to the thick carpet. "You've never said you were glad I'm here nor that you wanted me to stay."

Elizabeth pierced her with a stare. "You're my child. Of course I want you to stay."

"Thank you." On impulse Melissa threw her arms around her mother. She could tell she was stung but within seconds, her mother's arms awkwardly enclosed her in a brief hug. Melissa released her sliding back to her side of the sofa.

Elizabeth cleared her throat. Her eyes were brighter than usual but Melissa didn't comment.

"Well," her father said, "have you heard from Brent Sinclair in all these years?"

Melissa blinked at the question, confused for a moment but finally realized her father wanted to change the atmosphere in the room, to give his wife a chance to compose herself.

"I saw him for the first time a few months ago in Los Angeles."

"Really? Did he come to see you?"

"No, he was there on business."

"Hmm. I didn't know Sinclair Engineering had an office in Los Angeles."

"The Sinclair's businesses are diversified. You know that, Jasper. It's no surprise," her mother offered.

"I'm not surprised, Lizzie. Just curious."

"It was a chance meeting," Melissa said.

"You never did tell us what caused you to initiate the divorce," her mother countered.

"It was simple. Brent fell in love with another woman. I ended the marriage. Nothing more to talk about."

"He cheated on you?" Jasper roared.

"I don't believe physically but certainly emotionally. It was a long time ago. Brent and I talked and cleared the air. Five years ago, we didn't separate as friends. Now we're cordial."

"You're a young and beautiful woman, Melissa. You need to meet someone and start a new life. There will be quite few eligible men at the charity ball next month," Elizabeth snorted. "You'll have your pick."

Melissa stiffened, realizing that although she discussed aspects of her life with her parents, she left out her marriage to Jake. Her mouth opened but then she shut it. It had been three months since she'd seen him. The divorce would be finalized within a few more months.

Their marriage was short-lived just like her first one. Trust had been broken in both of them. The end of the marriage to Brent was a fleeting memory but with Jake it was still devastatingly painful, cutting deep each time she thought about it. It was as fresh as it was that night in his hotel room.

"Don't push, Lizzie. There's no doubt men will flock around our daughter. How could they not? She beautiful," her father said, while he leaned back against the cushion of his high back chair, and sipped his drink. "You need to get yourself a dress, baby girl."

"Thank you, Daddy. But I don't know if I'll be here."

"Why not?" Elizabeth asked.

"Well, I can't continue to live a life of leisure."

She wasn't going back to California. That was another topic for a different time. But she was seriously thinking about moving to Miami. She liked the city. Besides it was far enough from Jake for her to have a fresh start.

"You don't need to work, Melissa," Elizabeth insisted.

Melissa pressed her lips together, trying to hide a smile.

Elizabeth Delaney had a formidable personality. It was a part of who her mother was. She had come to accept it. She didn't want her mother to change—just to love her. And for the first time in her life, she was beginning to feel her mother cared.

"I enjoy working."

"Melissa, not counting our fortune, with the inheritances from my father and Jasper's parents, you're a very wealthy young woman."

"Please spend it on yourselves."

"We do, baby girl," her father chuckled, "but it just keeps multiplying."

"Real funny, Daddy."

"It's the truth."

"Why can't you do whatever job you do in California here in Dallas?" Elizabeth asked.

"Mother, it's not that simple. I'm a deal negotiator. It's taken me a long time to acquire the knowledge and skill."

"Well, I don't understand why—"

"Lizzie, let it go. Give her room to breathe." He winked at Melissa. "I believe our daughter will make the right decision for her...and for us."

Melissa laughed. "Daddy, you are a conniver."

He grinned. "Never claimed to be anything else."

CHAPTER FIFTEEN

The sun was just bursting through the window when Melissa woke. She lay in bed, listening to the birds greeting each other in their early day ritual. It was such an indistinct border between night and day. Stretching, sleep left her lazy but refreshed. The memory of Jake and the many mornings they spent in bed after making love surfaced. In the afterglow, their arms wrapped around each other, caressing. The talks about mundane things flittered through her mind. Then came the harsh reality of him in his hotel room with a half-dressed woman. Turning over, she burrowed beneath the duvet in search of the warmth that was missing from her life.

She swung her legs over the side of the bed and stood. A hot shower would clear her mind.

Dressed in a short-sleeve tank top and jeans she was ready to start the day. With forced pep in her steps, she made her way down the winding stairs to the kitchen. Another week had passed and Dallas was beginning to feel like home. It was January and the weather was nice. She was enjoying the new-found relationship with her parents. She fixed a bowl of cold cereal and fruit and headed to the patio

After she finished eating, she leaned back in the chair, tilted her face to the sun, enjoying the heat from the rays. It was so peaceful here.

No drama.

A call from her lawyer the evening before, informed her that he was still fighting the divorce. She was neither glad nor angry about his actions. More confused. Why was he doing this? Nope. Jake would stay in a silent compartment today. It was a lovely, warm morning with clear skies. There were no clouds in her life today.

The parents were out of the house. Her father was playing golf and her mother was at a breakfast meeting for one of her clubs. Sarah had gone to do the weekly grocery shopping and errands.

She loved her parents and the attention they'd showered her with but it was so nice to have the house to herself. She grabbed a book from the library and was headed back to the patio when the noise of the doorbell chimed throughout the house.

Without looking through the small privacy window, she threw open the door. Jake Sorensen stood before her. He was wearing a white silk shirt, which contrasted against his tanned skin. Black jeans molded the contour of his thighs. His jet-black hair was ruffled and sparkled with the sun from drops of water—as if someone had sprinkled fine gems over his head, though clearly he had just come from a shower.

His gaze flicked up and down her body, causing a reaction in her that angered her. She wanted to be over him. He studied her for one long, unhurried moment then the cold gray eyes hardened and he threw her a deep frown.

"Hello Melissa," he said smoothly. The sexy, roughness of his voice caused a sensation to cruise through her vagina. Damn. She didn't want to be affected by him.

Not waiting for an invitation, he stepped over the threshold into the house. She automatically fell back, allowing his entrance.

"Jake? What are you doing here?" She slammed the door.

His gaze narrowed and he studied her. "Is that all you can say after three months of no contact?"

Melissa eyed the dark arrow of hair revealed by the few shirt buttons which had been left unbuttoned and remembered the rush of desire that had overridden everything else, even sanity, in their relationship.

"There was no need to talk or see each other. I want you to sign the divorce papers."

There was a split second of a pause. "I could," he agreed. "But I'm not going to."

His expression was empty. The lack of emotion angered her.

Something told her he was playing a game but she refused to let him see how unnerved she was by his presence.

His mouth flickered in the mockery of a smile. "You're ready to talk now?"

"If that's what it takes to end this farce, then I will." She walked away, knowing he would follow. She entered the drawing room. He touched her, running his fingers down her arm, causing her to turn and face him. Melissa was aware of some unknown emotion clinging in the air about them—something unspoken and dangerous.

She inhaled a quick breath and wondered if he noticed. Jake was a maestro when it came to women. Did he realize how disturbing such a simple gesture could be—especially when she had been deprived of physical contact most of her life from the people who mattered? Was he deliberately trying to make her aware of how close they were to each other? She didn't want it. Did she? No—not ever again to tremble with passion and desire.

"I want you to sign the divorce papers, Jake."

"No."

"What do you mean no?" she questioned, confused by his answer, but she continued to exhibit a calm she didn't feel.

"Exactly what I said. No. We're married and going to stay that way."

She rubbed at her temple and stared at his powerful form and realized she was holding on by a thread. She wanted to scream, rant and curse at him. Being strong was one thing—but who could say how long she'd be able to remain so?

"You have lost your mind." She hated the tense and forbidding mask that seemed to have tightened his handsome face at her words. "I'm getting a divorce with or without your consent."

"Not going to happen. I admit I screwed up—big time. We'll get through this together. What happened in New York was nothing. I didn't have sex with that woman."

Melissa was taken aback by his distorted rationale for his actions. She would no longer operate within the strict emotional boundaries he seemed to dictate.

She decided to take charge of the situation. "How did you find me, Jake?"

"It doesn't matter. Just know that it wasn't easy."

"I didn't want to be found, Jake."

"So you admit you were hiding? Running like a scared rabbit from an adult situation. This mess started with your obsession with your ex-husband. I—"

"This was about revenge?" She shook her head in disbelief. "You wanted to hurt me? Get back at me for something your twisted mind conjured up about me and Brent? You are bitter, angry, and delusional."

He flinched as if she had struck him, staring at her. "You dare to call me that? You dare to not take accountability for the roller-coaster you put us on?"

"I will not take responsibility for what you did. I didn't sleep with Brent in his hotel room or anywhere else. You purposely brought your whore to your suite to have sex."

"I—"

"Don't say a damn word! The smell of her was all over you and you weren't backing away from it," Melissa cut in, mad as hell.

She could endure a lot but she wouldn't abide lies. With the revelation came the realization of just how weak and compliant she'd been all along—always accommodating, first with Brent and then Jake. No more. She loved Jake but she would live without him. She wouldn't be a doormat to any man—not again.

She didn't like the way she'd been treated by Brent but she'd also used him to get away from her parents. She realized now that all her life what she wanted most was to be cherished and loved. She was no longer that girl.

"How many times do I have to tell you nothing happened? But you couldn't stay around to listen to my explanation?" he taunted.

"Why should I? I saw enough. You're very good, Jake—I'll admit that. You would've smoothed over everything, making me believe what I saw was a huge mistake. Not many women can resist you, not even me. I should've known what we had was too good to be real." She felt the tears swell but she choked them back. "But at least we both know now where we stand—I want you to leave. Go back to Los Angeles. Sign the damn divorce papers. It's over. Let it go."

His dark brows elevated in a thin veil of disbelief. "I've been searching for you for months. When you were seen in Miami, I flew down, hoping to find you but you had left again. Then I received a call from the investigators telling me you booked a flight to Dallas—using your credit card. Not being a religious man, I prayed and thanked God for the favor."

"I forgot to use cash instead of a credit card. A mistake that won't be repeated," she said flippantly, in an effort to hide her surprise at his admission that he searched for her.

"I'm glad you did."

"Jake—"

"Although, I didn't invite Bridget to my suite, I didn't dissuade her either. I'm not making excuses for my behavior. It was deplorable. I can contribute it to pride and ego. This thing with Sinclair had me—"

"Melissa, we didn't know you had company." Elizabeth Delaney and her husband stood in the doorway and then entered the room.

Her mother kept her eyes trained on Jake as she moved closer, followed by her husband. When she reached them her eyes widened as she thoroughly examined Jake.

"Are you going to introduce us, baby girl?" her father said.

Jake looked at her.

"Mother, Daddy, this is Jake Sorensen."

Her mother held out her hand. "It's nice to meet you, Mr. Sorensen."

He shook her hand gently. "Please call me Jake."

After shaking Jake's hand, her father asked. "How do you know our little girl?"

Jake turned again to her, but remained silent.

"He's my boss, Daddy."

"And her husband," he said.

Oh, boy. What she would have given to disappear at that moment. Damn Jake. He was trying to push her into a corner. Both parents stared at her as if they didn't know who she was. Her mother was the first to recover.

"Her husband? Melissa didn't tell us she was married...again. When did this happen?" Elizabeth's words were curt.

"Six months ago," Jake said. "Before you ask any more

questions, Melissa and I have been separated for the last three months. I came to Dallas to settle our disagreements and bring her home."

"Do you think that's going to be easy, Mr. Sorensen?" Her mother's tone was hard.

"No, I don't. Nothing with your daughter is easy. She's no pushover." Jake glanced at Melissa. "I have my work cut out for me. But whatever it takes, I'll do it."

"Melissa is a strong woman. She has her father's brains and my tenacity. She's been through a lot and survived." Elizabeth stared him down. "Whatever the outcome between you and her, it's her decision. She'll not be alone. Not ever again." She paused for a moment, still staring at him. "Do you understand me, Mr. Sorensen?"

"Yes, I do. Melissa is my wife. I'll take care of her. She'll never want anything. I'll always protect her even if it's from myself. Do I make myself clear, Mrs. Delaney?"

Her mother stared hard at him for a long moment. The tension was thick. Finally, she said, "Crystal."

Melissa's head bobbed back and forth between her mother and Jake. What in the world had just happened? There was a strong undercurrent in the room that only those two understood. Each seemed to have laid down their gauntlets—at least for the time being. And when had her mother become her ally? Strange.

Her father looked at Melissa with sadness. "Why didn't you tell us about your marriage, Melissa? We are your parents. I thought we were making progress."

Melissa glared at Jake before addressing her father. "I'm sorry, Daddy. I didn't want you and Mother to know I'd failed at another marriage."

Her mother pursed her lips. "It's not a failure. It takes strength and courage to leave a marriage that's not working."

Melissa warmed at her mother's praise.

Jasper scrutinized Jake for a long moment. "You said you came to Dallas to get Melissa?"

"Yes, I did."

"Why?"

Jake's eyes darkened with anger. "Excuse me?"

"My daughter left the marriage. So, I ask again, why are you here?"

"Melissa is my wife. She belongs with me."

"This isn't the dark ages, Mr. Sorensen. You can't make her go with you against her will," Elizabeth said coldly.

"No disrespect. This is a private matter. We'll *solve* it together."

"Those are mighty strong words. I don't know you. But our daughter has a good head on her shoulders. If she left you, there was a reason. We'll stand behind whatever she decides to do."

"I understand, Mr. Delaney. But I won't lose her." He paused for a moment. "She's my world."

Melissa's eyes widened at the words coming out of Jake's mouth. She'd never heard him talk like this before. What was wrong with him?

"It's been three months, what took you so long to come for her?" her father asked with a frown.

After another pause Jake said, "I ran into some business problems. It took a while to settle everything."

She shook her head at how easily he lied.

Elizabeth pointed to a chair. "Please have a seat Mr. Sorensen"

"It's Jake, ma'am."

They all sat down.

Melissa's mother continued to observe Jake with a fierce intensity. But somehow hers seemed more analytical instead of admirable. Elizabeth Delaney wasn't deterred by a handsome face.

Jake's rugged good looks made him a stand-out in a crowd.

Being in the presence of a few people didn't diminish his appeal. Both parents were captivated. He dominated the room as if he were lit by some foreign inner fire. Her parents' eyes were drawn to him like a magnet. It didn't faze her.

"Would you like refreshments, Mr. Sorensen?"

Melissa spared a peek at her mother. She was always the gracious hostess.

"He's not staying, Mother. He was on his way out when you and Daddy arrived."

Jake's icy gray stare seared a hole through her. He looked as if he could strangle her. It gave her a measure of satisfaction to know she had him riled.

"He just got here," her father said, "It's nearing lunchtime. Our Sarah is one of the best cooks in the state of Texas. I can guarantee that whatever she's preparing today will be delicious. Besides it's about time we learn more about our son-in-law."

"Jake has a plane to catch, Daddy," Melissa interjected.

"No, I don't," Jake countered. "I can stay for lunch. I want to get to know my wife's parents."

Melissa shot him an angry stare.

Her mother stood and observed them for a long moment.

It seemed like an eternity to Melissa.

"Good. Then it's all settled. Sarah should be back from her errands. In the meantime, I'll check on lunch. I'm sure you and Melissa have plenty to talk about. My husband and I have questions but we will leave them for now." She started toward the door, stopped and lifted a brow at her husband. "Are you coming, Jasper?"

Melissa intercepted the silent message between her parents and saw the imperceptible nod her father gave.

He got to his feet. "Please excuse us." They walked out of the room together.

The silence had Melissa's nerves strung to a screaming point.

She jumped to her feet and started to pace. Although his eyes bored into her every movement, she refused to look his way.

"Leave, Jake."

"No."

"What was that back and forth banter going on between my mother and you?"

"A message of understanding."

She stopped and turned to him. "What does that mean?"

"Nothing for you to worry about."

"Forget it, then." She took a long deep breath and exhaled, counted to five, and planted her hands on her hips. "You're in my parents' home. I refuse to make a scene. I want you to walk to the door, open it, and go through it—now."

She said the words slowly as if she was giving directions to a small child.

He stood and advanced toward her. "Why didn't you tell your parents you were married?"

She refused to answer. "Go!" She found she was losing control quickly. Melissa hurried to the door of the drawing room and waited for him to catch up. He took his time to reach her. He stopped in front of her, staring into her eyes as if he was dissecting her thoughts. It made her uncomfortable but she refused to fidget. She glared back.

"Calm down," he commented, "you can get the idea of me leaving out of your pretty head. Do you think I came all this way for nothing? When I leave the state of Texas, you'll be with me."

"You're delusional. This isn't a game, Jake."

"No. It's not," he said, earnestly. "Let's sit. We'll continue our conversation like rational adults." He escorted her to the chair in front of the loveseat. He took the sofa.

"There's nothing left to—"

"I believe there is."

"Alright. You found me. Our marriage is over. Sign the damn divorce papers and end this farce."

"You can't get rid of me that easily."

"Dammit, Jake. Why are you being difficult? You're the one that cheated."

"I admit to fucking up. I didn't cheat."

She rubbed at the tension in her eyes and temple. The man was driving her crazy.

He had taken a position on the sofa, reclining like this was his house, hands behind his head and his feet stretched out comfortably in front of him. He was relaxed and she was pissed.

The sun was beaming through the windows, casting a beautiful glow into the room. But all she felt was dark anger and resentment seething through her, for him showing up when she was trying to forget him, turning her world upside down, and mad at herself for still loving him. She couldn't help that her eyes were riveted to the powerful reality of his physical presence. Disgust cruised through her. She didn't want to be aware of him or affected.

"I have a lot to say, Melissa, but your parents' home isn't the place for us to have an intense discussion." He stood and extended his hand. "Come with me."

She remained seated. "I'm not going anywhere with you."

Jake approached her, his face a stern, unsmiling mask. "I believe you will, Melissa. You went to great lengths to keep our marriage from your parents. I don't believe you want our discussion in front of them. Do you?" He smiled, but it didn't reach his eyes. "Well, if you do, I can accommodate you. But they'll know all of it, my love and I *mean all of it*.

"Are you blackmailing me?"

His gaze was chilly. "We need privacy. Then you can rant, scream and shout at me as much as you want."

"I need to let my parents know we are leaving."

"I believe they'll get the message. They know we want to be alone. But if it'll make you happy go ahead and tell them."

She left the room.

In the car, she maintained a steady silence for a long time, looking at the passing scenery.

"Where are we going?"

"Somewhere private"

She rolled her eyes. "You already said that, but where?"

"I've never known you to be impatient, my love."

"Stop it."

"What?"

"I'm not your love."

He glanced at her, but didn't say anything. But she could tell he was perturbed by the tightening of his lips.

Within forty-five minutes, they entered a driveway between laced black iron gates and wound alongside a tranquil creek to a grand entrance. The circular drive featured an Italian fountain studded with fire torches. The home's sandy stone veneer and steep slate roof with shades of green and blue gave it a sense of great age and timeless style.

"Where are we?" She continued to look at the beautiful grounds.

"Home."

Confused, she turned to him. "Home? This is your place? I didn't know you owned a house in Dallas."

"Now you do."

"How long have you had it?"

"Almost a month."

"Have you been in Dallas that long?"

"No, I arrived here three days ago."

"What is this about? Why here, Jake?" she insisted. "As far as I know you don't have any business in Dallas."

"I have plenty of business in this city."

She squinted. "Since when?"

"Since you came here." Those cool gray eyes pinned her to her seat, making her remember places and times when they were intimate. It stirred up all kinds of images she wanted left buried.

"Let's go inside." He opened the car door. "We won't be disturbed here."

Chapter Sixteen

Although the outside of the house was stately and beautiful, the inside was much larger. The entry hall was coated with gold leaf and accentuated with timeless fixtures of nineteen century pieces mixed with modern decor. They walked into an unbelievably huge room. She couldn't tell what type of room it was, family room, a great room or living room. A classic Baccarat chandelier hung from the octagonal coffered ceiling.

Against the backdrop of walls clad in Venetian plaster, alternating flooring of hand-scraped herringbone made the room breathtaking. Polished marble led the way through the room fusing, old architecture and modern conveniences together.

Lost in the majesty, she said, "This is beautiful, Jake."

"I'm glad you like it."

"I love it. This house has so much character. It's inviting and warm."

Without making a sound, a woman dressed in a maid uniform appeared in the doorway. She threw Melissa a quick glance but returned her gaze to Jake.

Jake frowned at the woman. "Yes?"

"Mr. Sorensen, Cook has prepared chicken Caesar salad and a cold tomato and corn soup for lunch."

"Leave everything in the fridge. My wife and I will help ourselves later.

The woman didn't even blink at the word wife. "Yes, sir."

"Please make sure we aren't interrupted. Better yet, you and the rest of the staff may leave for today."

She nodded and disappeared as quietly as she came.

"You have a staff already?"

"Staff came with the house. I saw no need to release them."

"How many?"

"A gardener, cook, and housekeeper."

"Your house is a mansion. You need more staff.

"The domestic help comes in four days a week. No one lives in. If you want, you can hire more staff."

Shock rendered her speechless.

He made straight to the bar and poured mineral water into two glasses, adding ice to one of them.

"Sit," he said, without bothering to turn. "The sofa is new but comfortable."

Melissa tried to maintain an indifference she wasn't feeling.

He handed her a drink. Her hand gave a slight tremble as she took the glass. To cover it, she drained the water in one long swallow.

"You want more?" he asked.

She shook her head and set the glass on the marble table beside her. Linking her fingers together, she inhaled fortifying breaths and then released the air in her lungs. The heat of his gaze warmed her skin; causing tingling in places she didn't want. She shifted in her chair, trying to get comfortable.

"You're restless?"

She stopped moving. "No."

His gray eyes roamed her face, finally holding her eyes captive.

"Since we are here, let's get on with it." Irritation laced her voice.

He frowned. His direct hold now was curious.

The stoic pressure of silence jammed the room.

She braced herself determined not to let him see her sweat.

Abruptly, his eyes turned heated. Aroused, a soft gasp escaped through her lips. She swallowed, hoping he didn't notice.

He smiled. "Are you alright?"

She cleared her throat and ignored the question. "We're at a standstill, Jake."

"I've made some mistakes with you, Melissa. I don't look back with regrets but I had to with you. I didn't give you a chance or rather I wouldn't listen to your explanation about Sinclair. I contributed to us heading down the road of mistrust and miscommunication."

She didn't say anything, waiting for him to continue.

"You're the most important part of my life."

She rolled her eyes.

He ignored it. "When it comes to you, I'm not myself...I lose focus." Jake commented calmly. "But, you're a different woman from when we started dating."

"Change is evitable. People grow. What do you want from me, Jake?" she said in a dry tone. She was tired of the merry-go-around and wanted to get off.

"For you to give our marriage a fighting chance. It won't survive without the both of us contributing."

"You believe there's something to save?"

He nodded.

She shook her head. "There's too many wounds, Jake," she said wearily. "Sharp words between us have cut deep. There's a lot of infection."

"We can start fresh today. Then the healing process can begin. All you need to do is let go of the anger."

Who did he think he was? He thought he could make the rules, demand she kneel and come back. Like hell she would.

"You're still a domineering, controlling, son-of-a—" She stopped herself before completing the sentence.

The atmosphere in the room shifted in an instant.

"You knew what I was before you married me." He uttered the words in a gruff tone. Those hypnotic gray orbs of his grew stormy and cold. She could see his multifaceted brain shifting into specialized compartments. He remained stoic, not releasing her from his mental grip.

Holding her composure, she fought not to show any emotion.

"I knew you were ruthless but not a cheating bastard."

"Damn, Melissa. You want to cut the jugular. This shit is becoming redundant. I'm not going to apologize for something I didn't do."

She came slowly to her feet. "But you wanted her, didn't you? Admit it," she screamed.

"Is that what's bothering you?" He pushed to his feet. "The thought of me with another woman?" He reached for her, ran a finger along her cheek and whispered in her ear. "Touching another woman. Giving her the ultimate pleasure I always gave you? Maybe you imagined finger-fucking...her swollen lips engorged. Or my tongue lapping at her juices as I bring her to a powerful orgasm," he taunted.

Hurt and shocked, she stumbled back into the chair behind her.

"Damn you Jake, I hate you."

He moved so swiftly she didn't see it coming until his fingers grabbed the tops of her arms, pushing her back against the wall.

"How could you?" Tears clogged her voice.

"I'm sorry, baby." He wrapped his arms tightly around her. "I'm so sorry...Please...I gave you the words you wanted to hear, not what happened. We need to stop hurting each other."

"You can be very cruel, Jake. I don't believe you know how to be anything else."

She pushed at his shoulders.

"Don't." He didn't release her. "You disappeared. You ignored my calls and texts. I was angry. Reckless."

"Your ego was bruised."

"It's more than that, Melissa. You sic that barracuda of a lawyer on me, thinking I would yield. It pushed me over the edge."

"I didn't—"

"Hell, will you *please* listen to me—"

"I'm tired. It's useless." She tried to pull away from his hands again.

His powerful body pressed hard against hers and she felt the familiar curl of excitement low in her belly. The instinctive response sickened her. Even now her body failed to recognize the man that he was. She tried to move again but he planted his hands on her shoulders, blocking an escape.

"Melissa. Dammit. I've given you three months to tackle your demons and come to your senses. This back and forth shit to see who can get the highest score isn't us. We went into this marriage wanting the same things."

"You don't know what I want."

"Then tell me."

She shook her head. "It's too late."

"No, it's not. You're the balance in my crazy world."

"Am I supposed to be flattered? You're still an A-class bastard."

"You're as bad as Sheila with your mouth. I've never heard you curse so much."

"Get used to it."

"No problem."

"You know what I meant."

She felt the tension pulsing through him and wondered with a flicker of shame whether she'd gone too far.

"Listen to me," he said. "Or so help me you won't like my methods."

"Are you threatening me?"

Their eyes clashed and the air surged tight around them.

"I can be a bastard. But you know I would never physically harm you."

She sighed. "I know. I'm sorry I implied you would."

"There are more enjoyable ways."

She had a feeling she wouldn't like his methods, which would probably include them intimately touching, something she wanted to avoid at all costs. *Liar,* her brain screamed. She remained still, waiting for him to continue speaking.

"I'll keep saying it until you believe me. I. Didn't. Cheat. On. You."

The flat simple but strong statement ignited a flicker of hope within her.

"You hurt me, Jake," she whispered. Her knees sagged and she would've slid into a heap on the floor if he hadn't caught her.

"I know, baby. I'm not making any excuses," he said in a raw tone. I'm not a demonstrative man. I'm conceited, I'm an ass-hole, I'm—"

"Yes, you are." She agreed. "I married you believing we had something that worked. You wanted a wife. I wanted to be lo...to be needed. We both wanted children. The business was an added bonus we enjoyed. We had friendship, sexual attraction... Then I realized the only things that interested you were power, money, control and your ego. We were supposed to be partners—"

"We are." He took her hand in his and held it close to him, staring deeply into her eyes. "You and I fought so hard to pretend the only thing we shared was business and great sex. But there's so much more. You're first in my life."

"I don't believe it. But, I can't deny the chemistry."

"I'm glad you acknowledge it."

"A marriage should be based on more than great sex. There's no love between—"

"That's where you're wrong." He inhaled a deep shaky breath and released it. "I do love you," he said with conviction.

Melissa watched him search her face for a reaction.

She stared at him incredulously. A lump settled in her throat. Tears gathered in her eyes, blinding her.

He ran a hand over the back of his neck and turned, stepping away from her.

His words vibrated throughout her brain over and over until it became a soft murmur. Shock held her immobile. She wanted to ask him to repeat it, but she was afraid she'd imagined his confession of love.

"I've loved you from the beginning. I thought I could be married to you and never tell you. Love wasn't something we discussed," he threw out in a soft tone. "I never wanted to fall in love...I didn't believe in it...until I met you."

"I wanted to believe what we had was enough."

"Now it's not?" he stated.

She remained silent.

"When I found out you'd been married. I didn't know how to deal with it. I saw the way   the two of you greeted each other. I was the outsider peering in a window at a scene that I wasn't a part of. I felt I'd lost you. But I refused to give you up because I was dying inside. I didn't know what to do to make you choose me."

"It wasn't a contest between you and Brent."

"You're in love with him," he uttered in a menacing tone. "That made it a contest."

"This is ridiculous. I married Brent because I loved him."

"You married me without love."

"Our relationship was different. It didn't involve a real connection."

He blanched.

She felt remorse at the callousness of how it must've sounded to him.

"I'm sorry. A riot of emotions are warring inside of me."

"Still?"

"Some. I carried a lot baggage from my past. I no longer have it."

"Sinclair helped you to come to that conclusion?"

"No. My parents. We have a long way to go but it's positive."

"Did you go to Sinclair when you left me?"

"What if I did?"

He flinched.

Why did she say it? Because she was afraid. Would she always wonder if she was enough? Could she live in anticipation of waiting for him to become bored and discard her? This man owned her soul—and he didn't know it.

"Jake, I didn't go to Brent. I can't change the fact I love him as a young girl and then as a woman. But it's over. We are now at the place that is good."

"What is that?"

"Friends."

"I see."

"I hope you do. But it doesn't change anything."

"I'm supposed to let you go?" he said, forcefully. "It's not something I can do. You're in my blood."

She lifted her brows into a frown.

"There are no other women, Melissa. Hell, I don't want another woman."

"You could've fooled me."

"Please...don't."

"You're a highly sexed man, Jake. Women approach you all the time."

"It has nothing to do with you and me."

She glared at him. "If they have the audacity to let you know they are available when I was with you—"

"I'm not available."

"Damn, the lines of women will be around the corners once you're single again." She sneered.

"Doesn't matter. I'm a married man and I will remain so. You are it for me, woman, only you."

Her beautiful brown eyes glistened with tears.

With a harsh expletive, he crossed the room and yanked her into his arms. "It's been a long time for me. I want you so badly, I'm trembling with need."

He stepped back. His hand shook as he held it out to her.

"No divorce...please." His voice was a low throaty grunt as he powered her against the wall again and trapped her there with the strength and heat of his body. "Since the first time I kissed you almost two years ago, you're the only woman I've made love to. I have been patient but I'm at the end of it."

"We can't settle anything like this, Jake."

Overwhelmed by his masculine scent, the fire in his eyes, she pushed at his hard chest, struggling with a temptation so powerful and potentially dangerous that her movements became frantic. "Let me go—."

"Never again."

She wiggled in an attempt to free herself and then gave a soft moan as she felt the hard ridge of his arousal and the warmth of his breath as his mouth captured hers.

"You are the most infuriating woman, but you're all *mine*."

"Are you sure?" she asked cheekily.

He leaned back and glared at her. "Definitely."

"That's a chauvinistic answer."

"Damn straight."

His mouth came down on hers with punishing force, his kiss ravenous and desperate, trapping her moans of need. She wrapped her arms around his powerful shoulders, her back pressed hard against the wall by the power of his body and the force of his passion.

She forgot her anger.

She forgot that this man had hurt her.

She forgot that she'd run from him.

She forgot everything except her need for him.

His kiss was a savage assault on her senses that destroyed all thought and willpower. She felt his hand slide up to cup her breast and she arched in a desperate plea for more.

He pulled the shirt over her head and threw it on the floor.

"I've missed you, Melissa...so damn much."

Her fingers burrowed into his hair.

"I need you," Jake groaned, his hands swift and determined as he stripped off her jeans leaving on her silk panties and she did nothing but urged him to continue.

She grabbed his shirt and jerked it opened in a rough, guttural gesture that sent buttons flying across the room. She opened the snap to his jeans, licking her lips in the process, and slid down the zipper, caressing his erection pressing against the front of his black boxers.

Then she planted the palms of her hands flat, pressing them against the muscles of his chest and dragged them down, over his rib cage to the top of his boxers where the shadowed line of groin began. She ached to free him, to hold his satin hard length in her hand, to stroke him, feel him, and then guide him into the part of her that throbbed for his possession. When she couldn't stand it any longer, she removed the constricting fabric, freeing him.

"Jake...the door isn't locked."

"No one is here."

"But—"

"Shh. No one will dare enter this room."

He lifted her to the high tabletop, their movement drawing her gaze to the mirror—their image sent a thrill of raw pleasure through her. There she was perched on the edge of pearl white marble, her hair in disarray, and her body humming with desire.

Jake sensed the thrill of desire that ripped through Melissa as she watched their reflection in the mirror.

He shifted her slightly and eased her panties from around her hips, discarding the scrap of lace before he settled between her legs again. He was immensely hard and he needed to be inside her. He loved this woman with every fiber of his being. She was as necessary to him as every breath he took.

He pulled Melissa forward. She gasped as her backside slid along the cold marble.

Nestling his hips between her thighs, his erection probed at the hot moisture at the entrance of her vagina.

"I can't wait, Jake..." Her voice was strangled. "Please—"

He slowed down. "I want it to be good."

"Damn you."

She was holding onto his arms, breathing erratically, her

breasts beckoning him. Her deep mocha areolas were tight buds, and he drew first one and then the other into his mouth. Her shuddering sigh of pleasure was almost his undoing as he wrapped her in his arms.

"It's been too long...I'm sorry. It's going to be a rough ride, sweetheart."

"Now. Jake."

"I won't be able to stop."

Her legs locked around his waist. "Do. It."

He entered her with a hard, possessive thrust that almost made him ejaculate. He held still and took deep breaths to calm his fast beating heart and the urge to pound relentlessly into her.

He watched her expression, and her eyes glazed. She'd wedged her hands on either side of his hips to keep her balance, using what leverage she had to flex against him, driving him in deeper. She moaned in response, and now helpless in his movements, he gave in to the rhythm his body demanded, his hips pumping hard and fast until her cries filled the room and her inner muscles spasmed around him. He continued to thrust deep until everything in him snapped. He lost it when she arched her back and her juices flowed around his penis. He felt the onslaught of a hard release but continued to pump deep and fast, bringing her to another shattering climax.

Finally, the pleasure was too much and it surged through him, shooting his semen into her body. All of it flowed into her womb and the overflow oozed down her thighs. They remained connected. He buried his face in her neck, muffling the aftershocks of such a powerful release that left him trembling against her.

"I love you, Melissa," he uttered against her skin.

She caressed his face.

He pressed a kiss into her palm and wrapped his arms around her.

Chapter Seventeen

After lunch, which also became their dinner, they called her parents to let them know she wouldn't be coming back that night. Jake thought the conversation had gone well. Although, there were a lot questions, some were answered, and others left for another time.

He and Melissa spent the rest of the day curled up in a lounge chair on the patio. Conversation had been cautious but flowed. Later, in bed, they made love several more times before falling into a deep sleep.

Jake woke to find his wife wrapped in his arms, their heartbeats beating in sync with each other. He didn't know what caused him to wake but he felt unsettled. What was the matter with him? Everything should be good. The woman he loved was in his arms. Fear edged the corners of his heart. How many times had he told Melissa he loved her during the day and night? Five? Ten? It felt good to him to finally speak what was in his heart.

The problem was Melissa never, not once, said she loved him. When he waited for a response, she remained silent or pretended she didn't hear him. It hurt—deeply. But he would give her time to learn to love him. Could he live with her never loving him? He had no choice. He needed her to breath. But the divorce still hung between them like a hundred tons of lava rock, with a red-hot boil beneath the surface.

"Go to sleep, Jake," she murmured against his naked chest.

He kissed her hair. "You're supposed to be asleep."

"I was until you woke me." She yawned, found a comfortable spot and returned her head on his chest.

"I'm sorry."

"It's your brain that woke me." She lifted her head; her eyes drowsy with sleep. "Something troubling you?"

"Us," he said without hesitation.

She shifted and lay beside him, not touching. Although only a few inches separated, he immediately felt the distance as if she was a million miles from him. He hated it, but he wouldn't ignore it.

He rolled to his side and propped his head in his hand. "What happened just then?"

"Nothing."

"Something did. Talk to me."

"Where do we go from here?" She paused. "Can we forget everything that has happened? I don't know if I can."

"I must be losing my touch." He tried to laugh but couldn't. The ache in his chest was increasing to unbearable pain.

"I'm serious, Jake."

"I'm not a sweet talker, Melissa. You know me better than that but I don't talk out the side of my mouth either. I told you I loved you and you didn't respond."

"I didn't come into the marriage with blinders on my eyes. I see you clearly."

"I told you I loved you."

"I know."

"And you didn't say anything."

"You're pushing, Jake."

"Damn, right I'm pushing. I'm fighting to win."

She sat up and glared at him. "You're infuriating, stubborn, arrogant, impatient, and—"

"Those aren't my only good qualities," he tried to joke.

He tried to tug her back into his arms but she evaded him and got up from the bed. She sat on the edge, reached for his discarded shirt and put it on.

"You're also ruthless." She threw the words over her shoulders.

"Ouch. That hurt."

"I didn't say it to hurt you."

He pulled on the jeans he'd dropped to the floor when they entered the bedroom. He walked to her side of the bed and took her hands. They moved to the loveseat in the corner of the room. She put up token resistance, but he allowed her to grudgingly maneuver into a spot beside him. He wanted her on his lap but thought better of it. She wasn't in the mood for it.

"How do you know you love me, Jake?" Melissa stared at him, holding his gaze. "You don't even trust me."

The question threw him but he paused before he spoke. His answers would need to come from the heart. He couldn't mess this up.

"I'm not sentimental, Melissa. I don't know how to be but being with you made me feel things I've never felt before. It's uncomfortable." He gave a short laugh. "To be honest, it scares the hell out of me. Trust comes hard for me. People always wanted something from me, whether it be my knowledge, money or my time. But you...hell, you didn't give a shit about any of it.

"You ignored me when I slyly tried to get you to go on a date with me after that first kiss." He paused for a long moment. "I do trust you, Melissa...with everything. For a time I let my foolish ego take charge and almost ruin the best thing in my life—you. I don't know the proper etiquette when it comes to love, nor am I a philosophical man. I never pretended to be. All I know is that I do love you." He stared at her. "I love your smile. The way you tilt your head especially, when you're thinking hard about something. Your laugh at the silliest things. Most of all, I like the way you plant your hands on your hips when you're getting ready to give me shit. I know we belong together."

"How do you know it's love, Jake?"

He placed his hand over his heart. "I know it here."

"I believe that's the longest personal speech you've ever made."

"I meant every word of it."

Her voice low and soft when she uttered, "I know."

He was afraid to ask but he needed to know. There would be no more misunderstandings.

"You hold all the power, Melissa. Your decision...Your choice."

She didn't say anything immediately.

"Would you let me go, Jake? Give me a divorce?"

The questions echoed in his heart like a dark, cold and empty cave. He swallowed the thump in his throat. Raw pain scaled his insides. With a fear so strong, he wanted to snatch her and lock her away with a violence that alarmed him. He wanted to pull her bodily and mentally into his world for her to see what he was feeling right now. His brain screamed no but his heart betrayed him.

"Yes."

"Why?"

"I love you, Melissa. I want us to have a life together but I want you to have the life you want more. If that means without me, then I'll sign the divorce papers."

She searched his eyes for several minutes and then got up from the sofa. With her back to him, she looked through the window out onto the darkened lawn. This man, whom she loved with all her heart, had just bared his soul to her.

An intensely private person, he wasn't accustomed to letting anyone see anything other than his hardness. Jake shied away from the word relationship. Their marriage had been a shell, smooth on the surface, but empty inside. Now he wanted to change the terminology.

She walked to him and held out her hand. He took it and stood. She allowed her fingers to trail down his bare arm and enclosed his hand with hers.

"Come back to bed." She tugged him forward. Then she released his hand and walked ahead of him. She stopped to make sure he was following, throwing a smile over her shoulder.

She tore off her shirt and scooted on the bed. He dropped the jeans he was wearing and followed her. He reached for her. Every touch of his hand, each look, drew her to him. She was almost delirious with need.

He licked his fingers, hesitated, and placed them at her entrance, working them slowly through the channel. She swallowed hard, moistening her lips with the tip of her tongue. She was almost there. At that moment, he removed his fingers, licking her essence from the tips.

He kissed her, entangling his hands through the dark locks of her hair, drawing her nearer. His every movement propelled her to entwine her body with his.

He latched on to a breast, worshipping it with his tongue and then the other one. Sexual electricity cruised through her, as powerful as any outside storm.

He lifted his head, staring deeply into her eyes. "I want you, Melissa. Just not for tonight but always. If it's not what you want, please tell me. We'll end it right here and now."

She pulled his face. "I love you Jake Sorensen. With everything in me, I do love—"

Before she could finish, his mouth captured hers in a deep kiss. Their tongues mated with each other.

Releasing her lips, his voice husky with emotion, he said, "I love you, Melissa Delaney-Sorensen. So damn much."

"Not Delaney-Sorensen." She smiled. "Just Sorensen."

"Whatever you want." His tone serious, he said, "There won't be a day that I won't tell you how I feel about you." The words were low and rough, as though he was not used to whispering. "Tell me again."

Melissa lifted a hand to his face and then hair. Savoring the feel of him beneath her fingers. "I love you."

He took her mouth, once again, with an urgent kiss of possession. Engulfing her in his arms, he pulled her into a savage embrace. She knew he was out of control and she absorbed it with a frisson of fear infused with excitement. She was powerless to resist.

"I must slow down...I want to make it good for you."

"It's already good. I want you."

"I have always been yours. Never doubt it."

"Jake..."

He pulled her to the head board and flipped her to her stomach. Automatically, she grabbed the headboard.

"On your knees," he uttered roughly. "I want to fuck you from behind."

She settled herself on her knees, trembling from anticipation. He buried his fingers into her and pulled her back to him, running his hand down her hip. She felt his penis at her entrance. She arched her back, pushing back against him.

"I don't want—"

"Now! Jake!"

He plunged into her.

A hard breath caught in her throat. He held his taut body still against hers. His breath escaped in a low hiss. Then he moved, plunging deeply, pushing her quickly to the edge. Her climax hit her hard, devouring her energy. He kept pumping.

"Melissa," he grunted and finally released his semen into the deep caverns of her womb.

Chapter Eighteen

A month later, Melissa packed the last of her clothes into the suitcase and set them by the bedroom door. The ritual was familiar and sad. It was time to head to the airport to be met by a private jet and fly home.

She looked around the room once again, opened the door and walked down the stairs into the corridor.

Jake stood with his cellphone to his ear talking, but also silently directing the workers to take certain pieces of furniture to the loaded van parked outside. Ending the call, he walked toward her.

"Are you finished packing, sweetheart?"

"Yes, the cases are by the door."

He spoke to one of the men walking by. "Could you bring down my wife's suitcases? It's the first room at the top up the stairs."

The man nodded and moved away.

Melissa wrapped her arms around Jake's waist and laid her head on his chest.

"I hate to leave."

"Sweetheart, we're not leaving Dallas forever. The house is ours. We decided to spend at least a few months a year here. Just for now, L.A. is our main base."

"I know and we agreed but I never thought I would ever want to live in Dallas again. But my relationship with my parents has changed how I feel."

He drew her to a deep leather wingback chair positioned near a window overlooking the rose garden and pulled her on his lap. She shot him a surreptitious look as she got comfortable. He groaned. Inwardly, she smiled, knowing he was aroused and there wasn't anything he could do about it. She should remind him that he was the one that chose to have her sit on his lap.

"I want you to be happy, Melissa. If moving us permanently to Dallas will do it, then so be it. It'll take time to transport the headquarters but it can be done."

Silence filled the room.

"You would do that?"

"For you, yes."

Tears filled her eyes. One escaped and ran down her face.

His eyes filled with concern, he stared at her. "What's wrong, honey?"

"Nothing is wrong. I was going to wait until we got settled in L.A. But—"

"You're scaring me. What is it?"

"I'm pregnant...We're going to have a baby."

She watched him with bated breath, waiting for the moment when the news finally connected with his brain.

His eyes widened with fear. "What? Are you okay? My God, Melissa, we had sex last night and this morning. It was—"

"Wonderful." She took his face in her hands. "Baby, we can have sex. It's not against the rules."

"Are you sure?" he asked sheepishly.

"Positive."

"I was a little rough last night. Maybe we should refrain from too much sex until—"

She laughed. "I'm not a fragile piece of glass."

"Okay. I guess I did get carried away."

"Are you happy?"

"Ecstatic. I didn't know it could get any better, but you have made me an extremely happy man."

She cleared her throat before speaking. Never would she doubt again his love for her. "I want my parents to have an active role in our child's life."

"Okay..." he said slowly.

"Jake, I don't want to leave L.A. Our life is there."

"Are you sure?" he asked.

"Absolutely. When we're not in Dallas, they can come to Los Angeles. You taught me to love again, Jake." She kissed him gently on his lips. "You've shown me that loving someone and allowing yourself to be loved makes you stronger." She smiled. "You even won over my mother, which is a very difficult thing to do. She loves you as much as I do."

He laughed. "That's a stretch. Your mother is a hard nut to crack. You never know what she is thinking. But she's warming up."

"Well, you have Daddy in your back pocket."

"That's because we hold you in the center of our hearts."

"That's a sweet thing to say." She kissed him. He tried to deepen it but she pulled back.

"There is nothing sweet about me."

She laughed. "I say it is."

"He grabbed her face and held it still. "I love you more each day."

To stop from crying with happiness, she placed her head beneath his chin.

"I love you very much, Jake," she murmured against his chest and then lifted her head to hold his gaze. "My heart belongs to you...only you.

"I know."

"You believe me now?"

"Yes. You're my life, Melissa. I love your strength, your fierceness...your laughter. There isn't anything I don't love about you. "

She would never get tired of him saying it. Melissa sighed with happiness. She'd finally found her place in life. She belonged to this man. Little by little he broke down the barriers she had put up for protection and she was glad he did.

ABOUT THE AUTHOR

Renee Wynn is a true romantic who believes in happy endings. A few years ago she read a romance by Brenda Jackson has been hooked ever since. Her first book, The Heart Knows, was chosen as a Top Pick by Romantic Times and the rest is history. This has encouraged her to continue the journey of writing about alpha males and strong heroines. Married to her college sweetheart, she resides in the Northeast.

Please visit the author's website at www.reneewynn.com for upcoming books.

Join her newsletter at www.reneewynn.com.